THE MASS. CENTRAL:

QUABBIN'S PHANTOM RAILROAD

By J. R. GREENE

Printed by Athol Press, Athol, Mass.

First Edition, August, 1996

1 3 5 7 9 8 6 4 2

ISBN 1-884132-04-9

The text of this book was set on the author's Leading Edge Model D word processor, using the Sans Serif type face.

TO DONNA

CONTENTS

Illustrations (From the author's collection unless otherwise credited):

James S. Draper p.7; Barre petition p.10; Belchertown milestone p.12; James M. Stone p.13; L.J. Dudley p.14;   Dr. Franklin Bonney p.15; Barre bond p.15; Central stock certificate p.18; Norman Munson p.20; Map of Mass. Central as pro- posed in 1871; p.24; Construction dumpcarts p.29; Luke Lyman p.32; Letter from James M. Stone p.35; Chester Chapin p.42; Cartoon on the Northampton bridge p.51; Silas Seymour p.55; Map of route change p.60; George S. Boutwell p.61; Locomotive *N.C. Munson* p.64; Waverly depot p.67; Hudson depot p.68; Waltham (North) depot p.69; Gleasondale (Rockbottom) depot p.70; Weston depot p.71; 1st Central ticket p.71; Wayland depot p.72; Central locomotive in Hudson p.72; Central pass p.74; Jefferson depot p.76;   1882 Central timetable pp.78-80; S.N. Aldrich p.83; Thomas Talbot p.86; West Hardwick culvert p. 95.

PREFACE

The story of the Mass. Central / Central Mass. Railroad was first recounted in a well-illustrated railroad history book* published in 1975. Unfortunately, less than one tenth of that book deals with the history of the line under its first guise, the Massachusetts Central RR (1869-83). While this part of the line's history lacks most of the "excitement" for a railfan of tracing the coming and going of various types of locomotives and rolling stock, it does offer fascinating sidelights on the politics of railroad formation and contruction.

Two reasons compelled the author to focus upon the Mass. Central project. The main one is that a large unfinished section of the line was flooded by the waters of Quabbin Reservoir (along with four towns and parts of several others) in the 1930s. The author has researched the history of that area since 1975, producing several published works on the subject. While the much more famous "Rabbit Run" (Boston & Albany RR, Athol Branch) is well known to Quabbin buffs, the story of the Mass. Central in that valley has been virtually forgotten.

The other reason is that parts of that unfinished and abandoned segment are still discernable east of the shores of Quabbin Reservoir in Hardwick. Many have hiked over portions of the "Rabbit" in the North Quabbin watershed, but few realize what that rocky little peninsula is that juts out from the shoreline of the Quabbin east of the south baffle dam.

The Massachusetts Central name was revived in 1979 by a corporation which operates the 23 mile-long former southern segment of the Ware River RR from Palmer to South Barre. Although this current line parallels the railbed of the old Central Mass. Division of the Boston & Maine RR north of Ware, there is no other connection between the two names. Therefore, that line is only briefly mentioned in this book.

The subject of this book is obscure enough to have caused this writer to engage in a rather lonely research job in compiling it. The corporate records of the Mass. Central are not known to have survived. Even pamphlets issued by the company are hard to find, except for a few from the late 1870s. This has caused a heavy reliance on newspapers and official documents from the period as original sources of information. These sources provide sufficient facts, and many revealing quotes from the participants in the events of the story of the Mass. Central.

Thanks are expressed to the following institutions for the use of their collections, reference materials and newspaper files: University of Mass. Library and Amherst College Library (both in Amherst), Athol Public Library, Barre Historical Society, Woods Memorial Library (Barre), the Baker Library of the Graduate School of Business Administration at Harvard University, the Commonwealth Archives and the State House Library (both in Boston), Clinton Public Library, Paige Memorial Library (Hardwick), Hudson Historical Society, Hudson Public Library, Swift River Valley Historical Society (New Salem), Forbes Library (Northampton), Palmer Public Library, the Essex Institute (Salem), the Connecticut Valley Historical Society (Springfield), Waltham Public Library, Worcester County Commissioners, Worcester Polytechnic Institute, Worcester Public Library, and the American Antiquarian Society (Worcester).

Individuals to whom thanks are due for their assistance include Richard Conard, Scott Czaja, Harry Frye, Mary Kelley, Melinda McIntosh, John A. Roderick, Jim Sullivan, Peter Taylor, Senator Robert D. Wetmore and staff (especially Genevive Frazier), former State Archivist Dr. Albert Whitaker and staff, and Stan Wonsek.

The Author
May, 1996

----
*The Central Mass, Boston & Maine RR Historical Society, 1975.

INTRODUCTION

In   the   hills of West Hardwick, one can find a disconnected series of cuts and   fills.   They are the monument to the uncompleted, and abandoned segment of a   railroad   that   was   to   connect that section and the Swift River valley with points as far away as Northampton to the west and Boston to the east.

As   one   newspaper   writer of the day aptly put it, the change of the rail-road's   route to the south would "doom West Hardwick to obscurity... leaving the unsightly marks of misdirected industry and capital to be of no earthly use ex-cept, perhaps, to puzzle the future antiquarian."

The Massachusetts Central Railroad was first projected in 1867 to serve many of   the   small   communities that were bypassed by the main lines of the Boston & Albany and Fitchburg Railroads. This "reason" for its construction was to con-tribute   to   the   delay of almost two decades to complete it. The need for this line   (or   potential business from it) in many of the towns along its route was not   strongly   perceived.   This made it difficult to garner stock subscriptions from   some of the communities on its route, and from private investors. Consid-ering   its   whole history, the authors of the B&M Historical Society's book, *The Central Mass.*, were correct in stating, in their Foreword, that it was "a rail-road that should never have been built."

In spite of these handicaps, the Central might have been completed in the early 1870s if it had not been for a run of bad luck. One large municipal stock subscription   had   to   be   voted on three times to get it right. A major deal to sell the line's bonds fell through because of a financial panic. The line's con-tractor   went   bankrupt   partly because another railroad owing him money went broke before paying him, and partly due to a sunken scow. The contract for the line's unfinished bridge over the Connecticut River involved a scandal investi-gated by the legislature. A banking house which was a major backer of the line collapsed because one of its managers got drunk at a bad time.

This railroad project engaged the attention of such important individuals as the   father   of   poetess Emily Dickinson, a former speaker of the Mass. House of Representatives,   a   former Mass. Governor, and a former U.S. Secretary of the Treasury (also a former Mass. Governor). It may have hastened the deaths of the first two, while being a low point in the career of the last one.

Even   though   its life as an operating railroad under the Massachuetts Cen-tral name lasted only about a year and a half, the political and financial intrigues behind it more than make up for a relative lack of good "railroading" stories.   The history of this line also proves that a large project like this, without a major financier behind it, was bound to fail.   The towns and politi-cians who conceived it could get any required state legislation passed, but could not obtain funds from Boston bankers.

Some of the facts revealed in this book will serve to clarify statements made in *The Central Mass* book. The emphasis here is on different personalities, in-cluding James M. Stone, Norman Munson, and others (some from the western towns on the line) who had more impact on the railroad's early career. Hopefully, this narrative will "complete" the story of this railroad's early years, as someday another writer may complete the history of the "end of the line."

Chapter One: A GREAT CENTRAL ROUTE

The route for what would later become the Massachusetts Central RR was first projected in the late 1820s. This was before any full-length railways had even been built in Massachusetts. The technology to construct railroads was developing, and a survey was commissioned to examine possible routes across the state. Engineer Loammi Baldwin surveyed several different routes from west to east.

The report on the survey prophetically proposed a "northern main route" that ran from west to east "...through Williamsburg to Northampton, thence through Hadley and Belchertown to the Three Rivers in Palmer; thence by the Ware River through Ware, New Braintree, Hardwick, Barre and Oakham; Rutland [to] Holden, West Boylston and Boylston, Berlin, Marlboro, Sudbury...to Cambridge."[1]   This route ended up being almost exactly the route of the railroad that was completed six decades later.

The report also included several possible "sectional routes." Route #10 was proposed to run from "Belchertown through Enfield, Greenwich and Hardwick to Barre; which would shorten the northern main route." This would later be the part of the railroad that was partially built, then abandoned before the whole line was completed. [2]

In 1835, the proposed Western RR from Worcester to Springfield was considering several possible routes to connect the two cities. There was much agitation in the Ware River valley about getting the route located there. A convention of concerned area townspeople was held at Hathaway's Hotel in Hardwick, on April 9. Those present passed several resolutions urging the use of a Ware River route. However, when the Western (later Boston & Albany) RR was built through that part of the state a few years later, it followed a shorter route through the Quaboag River valley to the south.

In 1848, a committee representing Enfield and Greenwich residents wrote to Constant Southworth and two other people from Hardwick. Southworth and the others were enjoined to raise funds "for the survey of a route for a rail road from Palmer Depot north."[3]   Southworth, a lumberman and box manufacturer, would obviously be interested in any improved way to ship out his goods. A public meeting was held to discuss this proposal. It must have been exciting, for one of the participants died on his way home! As in 1835, this agitation did not lead to any direct action. However, this episode may have helped to inspire a couple of railroad charters three years later.

Also in 1848, a charter was granted for an Amherst Branch RR, to connect that community to Northampton. This was encouraged by the recently opened Connecticut River RR, which paralleled that river north to south through Northampton. However, the existing line "withdrew its efforts to other quarters," and the opening of a line from Amherst to Palmer in 1851 "satisfied the immediate demands of [Amherst] for railway facilities."[4]   The Amherst Branch charter was revived in 1864 and 1868, making it a potential link in any "central" rail route.

In 1851, charters were given to three corporations to build railroads in the river valleys north of Palmer. Only one, the Amherst & Belchertown RR (now part of the Central New England RR main line) was built at the time. The other two, a Ware River RR and a Swift River RR, had Constant Southworth as a supporter. Due to an inability to raise funds, both of these projects had to wait almost two decades to be revived and built.

The nation embarked on a wild spree of railroad building after the end of the Civil War in 1865. This was led by the famous transcontinental project of the Central Pacific and Union Pacific RRs. In this atmosphere, many old proposals (such as the Ware and Swift River lines) were dusted off, and new ones sprang up to serve territories not yet on a rail route. Many of the Massachusetts communities located between the Boston & Albany and Fitchburg RRs felt the need for a more direct connection with Boston.

One of the many railroads proposed during that period was the Williamsburg & North Adams RR. Chartered on June 1, 1867, it was intended to connect Northampton, via. the Mill River valley, to the eastern portal of the Hoosac Tunnel (then under construction). There was a provision in its charter enabling the Commonwealth to loan this new line up to $1,000,000 toward its cost. That autumn, there was much discussion in Northampton about a municipal subscription of funds to support the line. Thus it can be seen that the idea of another route from Boston to "the west" (at least as far as Albany) was a possibility before the "central project" became developed.

Another one of the railroads proposed at this time was the Wayland & Sudbury Branch RR. It was chartered in February, 1868, to build a 6.75 mile line from Mill Village in Sudbury to Stony Brook in Weston (on the Fitchburg RR). One of the founders of this line was James S. Draper, of Wayland. Draper, born in 1818, was a farmer and surveyor, and a very public-spirited citizen. One of his notable civic accomplishments was helping to establish one of the first municipal public libraries in the state in his hometown in 1848. Draper served as its librarian for twenty years.

According to a biographical sketch of Draper published in 1890, he wrote a letter in 1867 to "a gentleman in Barre" (possibly Edward Denny) proposing "a central road through Massachusetts." It can be presumed that Draper had his proposed Wayland & Sudbury RR in mind as the eastern segment of this great scheme.[5]

Draper's letter stirred citizens of Barre to action, as they held "a large and spirited meeting" on the question "Shall Barre have a railroad?" on October 21, 1867. Edward Denny, a local industrialist, was chosen to chair the meeting, and was the leading speaker. A committee of twelve, including Denny, Hiram Wadsworth. J. Edwin Smith, and E.B. Shattuck were appointed to "confer with other parties and examine into the feasibility of the project."[6]

The town of Dana, just west of Barre, was the scene of the next railroad meeting, a little over a week later. A committee of fourteen men from Barre and Hardwick (including Constant Southworth) was appointed to persue the possibilities of carrying out the railway proposal. In late November, a similar

James S. Draper
(From *Annals of Sudbury, Wayland, and Maynard...*, 1891)

meeting was held in Ware; the resulting committee included industrialist Lewis Gilbert. The Ware committee apparently consulted with their counterparts in Barre soon thereafter, as they conducted a survey of a route between Ware and Northampton.

On December 8, 1867, representatives of the Barre and Ware committees met with citizens of Northampton at the Mansion House in that town. L.J. Dudley, a Northampton educator and state representative, was chosen the chairman. Those present discussed "an extension of railroad facilities east, by way of Ware and Barre, to Sterling Junction." The route east of Northampton was proposed to run south of the Holyoke Range through So. Hadley, Granby and Belchertown to the Ware River in Ware. While the Northampton people felt that the Williamsburg & North Adams RR was their top priority, they assisted in a subscription for a formal survey of the new line's proposed route.[7]

Even though the "central" proposal was discussed in some newspapers along the proposed route through that December, it seems that nothing further was done to push the project forward. Northampton was distracted from it by continuing debate over supporting the Williamsburg & North Adams RR, while Draper and his associates were busy getting the Wayland & Sudbury RR chartered.

As early as January, 1868, a letter writer to a Northampton newspaper, supporting the proposed Williamsburg & North Adams RR, felt that the latter line was an essential part of "a Massachusetts Central Railroad from Boston to Albany." While the short line connecting Williamsburg with Northampton would be built, the plans to extend it past Williamsburg to North Adams never came to pass. Northampton voted 532-421 against supporting it on December 9, 1868. At that meeting, the leader of the opposition stated that he would rather support a line heading eastwerd to Boston.[8]

The Northampton man's interest in a "central" project may have due to Draper again taking the lead with another bout of letter writing. This time, Draper could point to the Wayland & Sudbury RR charter as a start at the eastern end. Several public meetings were held in towns along the proposed route to discuss the proposed railroad.

Barre's meeting was held first, on October 16, 1868, with Edward Denny again in the chair. It was voted that "all interested parties unite in a petition to the next legislature for a charter for a railroad from Northampton to Boston, through the towns of Ware and Barre... to and over the present chartered road known as the Wayland & Sudbury Branch... to be called and known as the Massachusetts Central Railway."[9] A committee of fifteen people was appointed to carry out this mandate. It included members from Ware, Holden, and Sudbury, as well as Denny and Wadsworth of Barre, Dr. B.H. Tripp of Rutland, Francis Brigham and George Houghton of Hudson, and Draper of Wayland, all of whom would be among the petitioners (and members of the first board of directors) for this railroad.

This meeting received coverage in a number of newspapers across the state, which also discussed the prospects for the central route. The *Worcester Spy* called the project "a desirable one." Draper wrote an article about the meeting for the *Waltham Free Press*. The only negative comment on the project from a newspaper near the route was from the *Palmer Journal* (a Boston & Albany RR town), who thought "the prospect [for the line] is not... very promising."[10]

"The *Boston Advertiser* noted (somewhat incorrectly) that the proposed route of the line was "unaccomodated with railroad facilities," and that it would provide "more direct facilities for the great western trade." This combination of of elements was seen to "appeal... both to local interests, and to metropolitan commerce and capital," thus granting the project "due attention." [11]

The author of the *Advertiser* article failed to point out that the largest town on the proposed route without any current or projected rail service was Wayland, which had a population of only 1,776 people in 1875. Neither did he point out that the route was rarely more than fifteen miles from either of the existing parallel rail lines. These two points would later be seen as major handicaps to carrying out this project.

A railroad meeting was held in Enfield on October 23. A Dana man who was the chairman for the evening "made quite a favorable statement concerning the route," emphasizing the Swift River valley as a logical part of the line. Constant Southworth was among several speakers boosting the project. After arranging for a survey of their section of the route, they voted for a committee "to visit Amherst, Hadley, and Northampton to "stir up the people and awaken an interest in the matter."[12]

A meeting held in Amherst on November 2 found much enthusiasm for the project, provided it passed through that town and Hadley, instead of on the south side of the Mt. Holyoke Range. Funds for a survey were promised. The citizens of Hadley held "a large and earnest gathering" on the matter two days later, supporting a survey through their town.[13] The town of Bolton voted to support for the project at a towm meeting in early November.

Several representatives from the local committees met in Worcester in early November to co-ordinate their efforts. After the "whole matter was fully discussed," it was decided to "push things," and apply for a charter. William A. Gould, a Worcester engineer, who had surveyed a route westward from Oakdale, was engaged to survey the route east from that place to Sudbury.[14]

On November 4, 1868, a petition was filed with Secretary of State Oliver Warner to seek legislation for chartering the proposed central railroad corporation, to be capitalized at $3,000,000. The filing gained the favorable attention of many newspapers, including some in Boston.

Ironically, even though Enfield was listed as one of the towns on the line's projected route, no Swift River valley resident's name appeared on this initial petition! This lack of interest on the part of valley residents may be explained by the simultaneous attempt to charter the Athol & Enfield RR north to south through that valley.

The existing east-west lines in the state, the Fitchburg and the Boston & Albany RRs, were understandably opposed to the central scheme. However, their officers did not try to obstruct the passage of a charter bill. Newspaper editors from some of the towns along the established lines did express skepticism over the need for, or viability of, the proposed line. Problems arose from potentially rival schemes, such as the Amherst Branch, Ware River, Athol & Enfield RRs, and a Boston to Gardner line. These were either allowed an option to join in with the central project, or allowed to wither away (as did the last named).

A meeting was held in Amherst on December 30, 1868, attended by "about forty gentlemen from towns along the line." It appears that Northampton people had disputed with Amherst adherents of the project over whether to put the route of the line north of the Mt. Holyoke range (through Amherst) or south of it. Representatives of the two towns "smoked the pipe of peace" and agreed to work together to "put forth every honorable effort to secure a railroad between

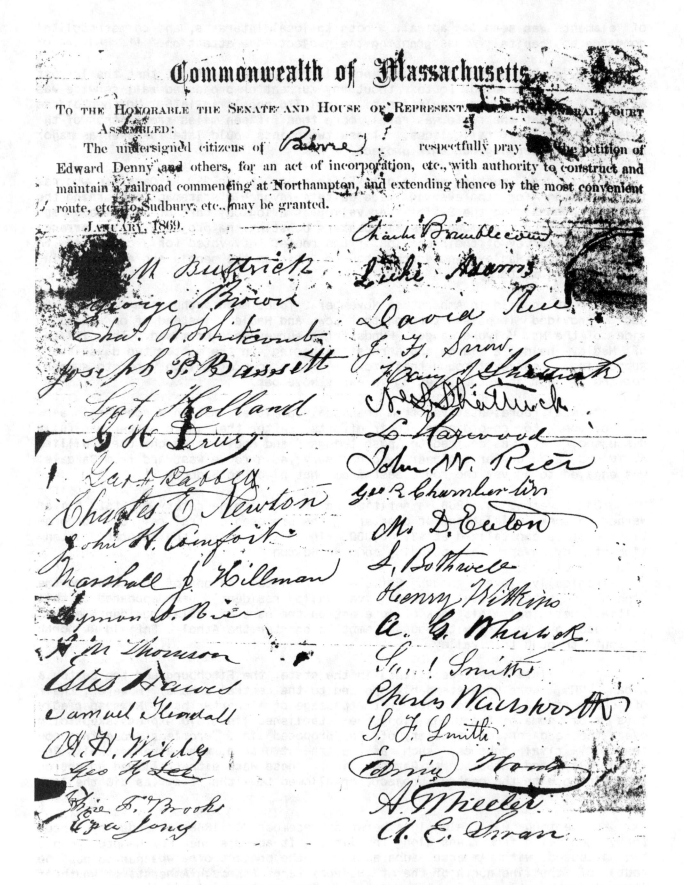

Commonwealth of Massachusetts

To the Honorable the Senate and House of Representatives in General Court Assembled:

The undersigned citizens of *Barre* respectfully pray the petition of Edward Denny and others, for an act of incorporation, etc., with authority to construct and maintain a railroad commencing at Northampton, and extending thence by the most convenient route, etc., to Sudbury, etc., may be granted.

January, 1869.

The front page of a petition for the Central railroad submitted to the legislature by Barre residents. (Mass. State Archives)

Northampton and Boston, at the earliest possible time, and on such route that surveys... shall show to be the best." The meetinmg appointed a committee of members from several area towns to aid in securing a charter.[15]

Meetings were held in Clinton, Lancaster, and Worcester during January and February, 1869 to whip up interest in the central project. Working committees were set up to get more petitions for the charter to the legislature. Engineer Gould was retained to make necessary surveys. It was at this time that a formal name for the line was adopted; the Massachusetts Central railway. [16]

As petitions in favor of the project piled up at the State House, proponents of the line set their strategy. A meeting, chaired by Edward Denny, was held in the Green Room of the State House on March 4. Engineer Gould's surveys and estimates of the cost of the proposed route were "found to be even more favorable than was expected." Many of the towns on the route were represented at the meeting, which expressed a "gratifying degree of harmony and confidence in the ultimate success in the enterprise." [17]

The legislature's railroad committee held its hearing on the charter bill on March 23. A "large delegation" from the towns involved was present to push the scheme. The only discord seemed to come from the presentation of rival routes between Northampton and Belchertown, and from Belchertown to Barre. This caused the hearing to continue into the next day. Upon the conclusion of that session, the petitioners were asked to prepare a bill for the chartering of the line. They got the impression from the committee that "there would be little doubt" of its being reported out to the whole legislature.[18]

Friends of the central railroad project met at the American House in Boston in early April. The progress of the bill was reported to be "fairly set agoing." Discussion centered on the prospects of getting towns along the route to subscribe for stock, which would be an important part of financing the project.[19]

The bill chartering the Massachusetts Central RR was passed on May 10, as Chapter 260 of the Acts of 1869. The line was capitalized at $3,000,000, with authority to increase this up to $6,000,000. In an attempt to be many things to many people (and to garner more legislative votes and stock subscriptions?), the list of towns on the line's potential route included many that were left out of the final survey. These were: Williamsburg, Easthampton, Westhampton, Hatfield, South Hadley, Granby, Ludlow, Ware, Palmer, West Brookfield, Dana, Petersham, Phillipston, Hubbardston, Princeton, Sterling, Clinton, Lancaster, Northborough, Stow, and Marlborough. A few of these towns would make sense only if they were considered as potential locations for branch lines.

Included in the provisions of the line's charter was the absorption of the Wayland & Sudbury Branch RR (which was done), and the option to unite with the Williamsburg & North Adams and the Ware River RRs. Other railroads intersecting its route, which the new line was authorized to make arrangements with included the New Haven & Northampton, Connecticut River, New London & Northern, Worcester & Nashua, Boston, Clinton, Lancaster & Sterling Branch, and the Fitchburg. While none of these potential combinations came to pass, this listing alone proved that the Mass. Central was hardly planning to traverse "virgin" territory.

After the central railroad charter was passed, another bill was filed to obtain a $3,000,000 loan for the line from the state. This concept was controversial, in part due to the bill's being filed late in the session. A weightier consideration against this new bill was the fact that the state had already loaned money to the Western (later Boston & Albany) and the Boston, Hartford & Erie lines, and to the Hoosac Tunnel project. Due to the lack of tangible returns on the second and third of these investments, many legislators were leery of committing any more state funds to rail projects.[20]

Newspaper editors chipped in their opinions of these loan bills. The *Springfield Union* called them "doubtful measures," and recommended that they be put off until the next annual session.[21] The *Springfield Republican* also objected to these bills, calling them "a desparate attempt to lobby and log-roll them through together." This paper called for the bills to be delayed, and thought that considering a loan to "a paper railroad," such as the Central, would not be in the interests of "economy" in the state budget.[22] The *Worcester Spy* also chimed in against the loan. Of course, newspapers from Springfield and Worcester could be expected to "labor to throw cold water on this [the Central] project... because it may divert some business from the Boston & Albany RR."[23]

The *Hampshire Gazette* of Northampton, for its part, called the *Republican's* dismissal of the Central as a paper railroad "sneering," and a sign of Springfield's prejudice in favor of the Boston & Albany. The *Gazette* called for the legislature to "give us all a fair chance" in consideration for the loans.[24]

A great deal of acrimonious debate took place over the Central loan bill as the legislature wound down toward the close of its session that June. Warm defences of the bill were made in the House by Rep. Crosby of Williamsburg, and by the representatives from Belchertown, Rutland, and Natick. The opposition, led by Rep. Plunkett (of Boston) made several points which seem now to have been prophetic. Plunkett pointed out that the valuation of the towns along the line was not enough to pay for building it. He also threw a dig at his Central Massachusetts colleagues by pointing out that, when pushing for state aid for New Salem Academy, they "almost shed tears over the barrenness of the region, but who now represent it as a very paradise." Another opponent asserted that "if the state had to turn the first sod, she would probably have to drive the last spike."[25]

As the *Springfield Republican* would chortle, the "ring railroad bill was defeated."[26] No state loan would be forthcoming; the bill to accomplish this was tabled to the next annual session of the legislature. The only government aid for the Mass. Central would come from stock subcriptions by towns along the route.

Old Milestone in Belchertown

Chapter Two: RAISING MONEY

The Mass. Central had a charter, but no money, and no corporate sponsors. It would have to organize a corporation to lay out its route, and raise the funds to build it. To do this, it would need directors from many of the towns on the route, including political figures and industrialists.

The corporation organized that summer, electing a board of directors in August. This consisted of James Draper, Francis J. Parker (a noted Boston broker and financier), Charles A. Cutting of Boston, Francis Brigham of Hudson, B.H. Tripp of Rutland, Hiram Wadsworth, Edmund Denny, and J. Edwin Smith (all of Barre), C. C. Aldrich of Granby, Lewis J. Dudley of Northampton, Joel Hayden of Williamsburg, and James M. Stone of Charlestown. This last member deserves more attention, as he was to become President of the fledgling line.

James Madison Stone was born in 1817, in Westford, Mass., the youngest of nine children. He left Westford in his mid-teens to work as a store clerk in Lowell. In his early 20s, he moved to Charlestown, Mass., then a separate municipality. He entered the field of journalism, and served as editor of the newspaper *Vox Populi* for six months in 1841. Two years later, he edited and published *The Herald*, which survived for only a few months. In 1850, he was publisher of the weekly *Democratic Standard*. This paper reflected Stone's free-soil and anti-slavery sentiments.

Stone was elected to a seat in the legislature by a coalition free soilers and Demcrats of Charlestown. He served in 1850 and 1851. When the Republican party formed in the mid-1850s, Stone reportedly "became influential in its councils."[1]

James M. Stone
(Mass. State Archives)

After giving up his newspaper in the early 1850s, Stone became a real estate broker, and was involved in several businesses. Stone invested in the Botolph Oil Well Co., serving as its President for a time in the late 1860s. He also served on the board of directors of the Broadway RR (in Boston) from 1863-65, and was also President of this in 1868. An historian of his hometown, writing after Stone's death, called the latter "one of the most effective men in influencing legislation, and was sometimes called 'King of the Lobby.'"[2]

Stone re-entered the political scene by regaining his old house seat for the 1864 and 1865 sessions. He ran for the speakership in 1866, beating out future speaker Harvey Jewell in a close contest. Stone was re-elected speaker in 1867, and was instrumental in the enactment of legislation to renovate and repair the State House. He was named one of the two commissioners (the other was Senate President Pond) to oversee the work, resigning his House seat to do so.

Several problems beset the project from its beginning. The bill authorizing the work omitted an appropriation of funds to spend, so the commissioners borrowed the money from the state treasury on their personal notes. This action was approved by the Governor's Council, and the Attorney General.

Although the original intent of the legislation was to have all the work on the State House repairs done under one contract, the two commissioners agreed that the only practical way to accomplish this was to award separate contracts for the different parts of the work. They also agreed that repairs not anticipated in the original legislation should be undertaken, which added to the total cost of the work.

A few months into the project, Commissioner Pond died, leaving Stone to supervise the work alone. Although Stone'e ability to act as sole commissioner was upheld by the Attorney General, he was criticized for appearing to act independently in arranging for some of the renovations.

Early in 1868, a legislative committee looking into the renovations concluded that Stone had exceeded his legal mandate in contracting for more work than had been originally intended. When it called him and the project's architect to personally appear before them, both men were out of the state (both later offering plausible reasons for their absences). The angered committee held up payments to some of the contractors, who blamed Stone for the delay.

Stone demanded a full hearing before the committee early in 1869, and this was held in March. After listening to numerous witnesses, and Stone himself, it concluded that no wrongdoing had taken place, and that all contractor's bills be paid. The committee applauded Stone for his "ability and integrity" in handling the difficult task.[3]

Exactly when, or for what reasons Stone became involved with the Mass. Central project is not known. His previous involvement in many business interests, including other railroads, would indicate a predisposition towards such a project. Stone's eminence as a former Speaker of the House, and the political connections which that entailed, certainly made him a useful man for the fledgling line to take on board. While the hearings on the State House renovations may have prevented Stone from becoming actively involved with the chartering of the line, he was "on board" early enough to be elected one of the original directors.

Four of the other Central directors merit some attention.

Lewis J. Dudley

Lewis J. Dudley was one of the longest serving Central directors. Born in 1815, he was raised on a farm in Connecticut. He graduated from Yale University in 1838, and later received theology and law degrees from there. Giving up law, He relocated to Northampton, operating an academy there for 14 years. In the 1860s, Dudley was elected to both houses of the state legislature. He was one of the co-founders of the Clarke School for the Deaf in Northampton.

Another important director was Hiram Wadsworth, a Barre native. Born in 1808, he was a businessman in the village of Dennyville for 27 years. In 1856, he went to Boston, and formed a mercantile partnership, Wadsworth, Crooker & Co. During the Civil War, he retired to Barre, and became a trustee of the Barre Savings Bank. Wadsworth's Boston connections, and his prominence in a key town on the Central route were assets to the line.

Franklin Bonney was from Hadley, near the western end of the line. Unlike many of the other directors, he was not in business, but a doctor. Born in 1822, he graduated from Dartmouth College in 1847, and set up a medical practice in Hadley. During the Civil War. he served as a volunteer surgeon for the Union army in Virginia. He was awarded an honorary A.M. degree from Amherst Col-lege in 1869.

Dr. Franklin Bonney

Captain Francis Brigham, of Hudson, was a shoe manufacturer. Born in Marl-boro in 1813, he was the founder of F. Brigham & Co., which employed 300 peo-ple making shoes during the Civil War. He was also a partner in the F. Brigham & Gregory Co. Brigham served his town as a Selectman at one time. He was a good man for the Central to have, as he could be both a fundraiser, and an investor in the project.

At a meeting on September 10, 1869, the board elected Stone President of the corporation. Other officers were James Draper as Clerk, and Francis Parker as Treasurer. Although scattered portions of the proposed route had been surveyed, the board wasted no time in commissioning a new, complete one. Edward Frost, brother of a supervising engineer on the Hoosac Tunnel project, was hired to carry out the survey. An office was obtained at 10 Pemberton Square in Boston.

The first major task for the board members was to solicit subscriptions from individuals and towns along the route. Barre was the first town to act, in Sep-tember, voting unanimously to take $90,000 in stock. Other towns subscribing by year's end were Rutland ($25,000), Hudson ($55,000), Berlin ($20,000), Wayland ($32,500, by a vote of 103-2), and Berlin ($20,000). Granby subscribed by a one vote majority, but was left out of the route in the final survey, thus neg-ating the subscription.

A bond issued by the Town of Barre to pay for its subscription to the Central.
(Barre Historical Society)

Subscriptions were also solicited from individuals. A portent of the Central's future problems may have been shown by its lack of support from any "private capitalists" of Boston. Some civic-minded people in towns on the route did subscribe for stock ($50,000 in Barre, and $36,000 in Wayland), but this was only a small percenatge of what was expected from municipal sources.[4]

On January 1, 1870, the *Springfield Republican* ran one of a series of articles on railroads in Western Massachusetts, focusing on the Mass. Central. The writer asserted that the line, "which exists only on paper... has great expectations, fair promises, and pressing necessities." He also pointed out that the line would have to cost much more than was projected, and that it would serve an area already crossed by several other lines. Edward Denny, one of project's early promoters, was quoted as saying "My interest in the enterprise has pretty much faded out, in consequence of the various complications in which it is involved."[5]* Such negative thoughts or statements were not surprising from a Boston & Albany town, so this elicited almost no comment.

Such naysaying did not stop James Draper from pitching in to speak in favor of a subscription. He showed up on the first Monday of that January at a meeting in the town of Weston to consider the town's taking stock in the railroad. In spite of Draper's "clear statement of the purposes and prospects" of the line, the town put off action, then voted to refuse to subscribe for stock.[7]

A few days later, on January 12, 1870, the first annual meeting of the Mass. Central RR was held in Boston. Since President Stone was absent (on a trip to London and Paris), B.H. Tripp of Rutland was chosen to run the meeting by the thirty men present. It was not deemed suitable to elect the directors for the year, so a committee of five was chosen to nominate members of the board at an adjourned meeting two weeks hence.

However, it was reported that Stone would "go abroad again shortly in the interests of the road," so that it could "apply in London for £ 4,000,000 ... to build and equip the road in the best style."[8] This may not have panned out, for the railroad filed a bill in the 1870 legislative session seeking state aid. The bill also sought authorization to build the road in sections, in order to continue if any shortfall in funding might occur.

Stone must have returned from his travels by late February, 1870, because he soon began an active campaign of speaking and lobbying for the Central. Among the many towns considering voting stock subscriptions to the line were the larger communities of Northampton and Amherst, on the western end of the route. One potential complication was the existence of a charter for the Amherst Branch RR, which was to connect Amherst and Northampton. Some people in those towns preferred to carry out this project, feeling it was more of a sure thing than the Central would be.[9] However, provisions in the charter of the Amherst Branch allowed it to be absorbed by the Central.

Stone spoke at several public gatherings in these towns in March. These were held before the town meetings that would vote on subscriptions of stock in the Central. One newspaper described Stone as "energetic," and as a man who "means business," while he made "a very favorable impression" on another. He "spoke with plainness and candor" to demonstrate that the Branch project would be "hostile" to the Central. This was true from Stone's point of view, because the Branch would have drained off the municipal subscription money from at least three Central route towns.[10]

----

*Confirming this, Denny later told Ginery Twichell (a director of the Boston & Albany RR) that he was "weary" of the Central.[6]

Stone's work was rewarded by votes to take stock by Northampton and Hadley in April. Northampton took up the matter at an adjourned town meeting session on April 4. Three hours of debate took place on the subject, led off by Charles Delano's motion to postpone the matter indefinitely. After this was defeated, a motion was made to subscribe for 3,000 of the $100.00 shares. This included provisos concerning the location of the route (north of the Mt. Holyoke Range) and Central's obtaining sufficient subscriptions before any payments could be made by the town.

Delano "labored with great zeal and ability to defeat the whole enterprise," but his advocacy of the Central when he was seeking support for the Williamsburg and North Adams RR project a year and a half earlier was used against him. Delano then brought up Stone's record during the State House renovations as evidence "of his want of capacity and trustworthiness." This "unwise" attack on Stone was "warmly" rebutted by a local businessman. When it was decided to vote on the motion by ballot, Delano tried to have this done openly, using the pretext of accountability, but this was deemed "inquisitorial," and defeated by a large majority.[11]

When the ballots were counted, the vote for the subscription was 562-247, a margin exceeding a two thirds majority. When he was informed of the vote, Stone telegraphed Northampton: "This day's vote secures the rapid and substantial advance of Northampton's prosperity. Let Amherst and Old Hadley promptly follow Northampton's noble example, and the Mass. Central Railroad will be completed as a through line within two years."[12]

Stone enlarged upon his point in a letter to the Northampton newspaper. He stated that the subscription by that town "will insure such subsequent town action as will enable the company to make a contract with reliable parties within six, possibly three months. to build the entire road... within two years. I have no doubt of it." Little did Stone know that this vote was not the last one needed to obtain Northampton's money. The editor of that newspaper urged Amherst and Hadley to give their "aye and amen" to subscriptions.[13]

Later that month, Hadley approved a stock subscription for $70,000 by a vote of 170-17. This included a proviso that the line go through Amherst. Having garnered subscriptions from a few more towns on the central and eastern sections of the route, Stone redoubled his lobbying efforts in Amherst and the towns east of it in early May. He succeeded in convincing Oakham (by a vote of 40-25) on May 7 to take $17,500 of stock. Stone tried to dissuade Enfield from supporting the Athol & Enfield RR, but was unsuccessful.[14]

In his drive to get Amherst to subscribe, Stone attended a public meeting there on May 14, accompanied by fellow director L.J. Dudley of Northampton, and Engineer Frost. Stone noted that the line was "not projected for private speculation," and gave other compelling reasons why the town should subscribe to stock in his line. He also stressed that a subscription would confirm the line's route into town, although it was known that Northampton and Hadley's subscriptions were based upon an Amherst route.[15]

In late June, Stone addressed a circular to citizens and newspapers in Amherst and six other towns on the route "in behalf of the thirteen towns which have already subscribed for the stock." Citing the experiences of the Boston & Albany and Fitchburg RRs, it asserted that the Central would pay dividends, and increase the business and population of the towns along its route, even those already served by a railroad (like Amherst) because of the direct connections with Boston and the west.[16]

Since Amherst took no immediate action on the matter, Stone proceeded to
Holyoke in early July to interest that city in connecting with the Central. He
attended a meeting of the Holyoke & Westfield RR in early August, attempting to
promote a branch line from Holyoke to Belchertown. Besides trying to scare
Amherst into action, Stone may have also been attempting to project his line
southwestward from Northampton (via a connection with the New Haven & Northampton RR), for such a scheme would be revived in the future.

Stone suffered a setback in West Boylston in July. When the stock subscription was first brought up early that month, the town voted 108-97 to take
$46,400 worth of stock. Opponents claimed that the meeting was attended by only
about half of the eligible voters, and successfully sought another meeting.[17]
This was held on the 20th, and voted to rescind the earlier action.

In early August, Stone went to Amherst to assist a local committee in arranging for a special town meeting for a subscription, and with the wording of
the necessary article. Later that month, he issued another circular, stressing
the lower costs of travel and freight for the towns along the Central compared
with current costs. Stone was reported to be "hovering about" Enfield late in
August, in another unsuccessful attempt to dissuade its citizens from supporting the Athol & Enfield RR.[18]

Amherst's interest in the Central matter became serious in late August, when
the town meeting to consider the subscription was set for early September. The
town's weekly newspaper supported the subscription; only one letter writer opposed it before the town meeting in early September. "Taxpayer" felt that the
town could not afford the subscription, and that the New London & Northern RR

A Massachusetts Central stock certificate

provided the town with adequate railroad facilities. He prophetically predicted that the town would never get any dividends from Central stock. The newspaper's editor took pains to rebut these views, pointing out that, with bond-
ing, Amherst could well afford the subscription, that the Central's direct connections with Boston and Northampton would aid local business, and that the Central would pay dividends because it was not a branch line.[19]

Stone attended a public meeting on the Central issue held in Amherst the
night before the town meeting. He promised that the construction of the line
would be contracted for within a month if Amherst subscribed for stock. Stone
asserted that the Ware River RR and the Boston & Albany RR were in opposition
to the Central, the latter not wanting Amherst to have its own route to Boston.   One observer noted that "Mr. Stone's arguments were convincing to those
who were wavering in mind as to the policy of helping the road."[20] Central director Franklin Bonney, of Hadley, also spoke in favor of the subscription.

The Amherst town meeting held the next day had an "unusually large" crowd.
A newspaper reporter thought that the opposition was swelled by many who "had
been drummed on to defend themselves from what they deemed an attack on their
purses."   When the time came to discuss the railroad question, those opposing
it sought to have the vote taken by ballot, but this failed. The reporter felt
that this method would have insured the railroad's success.

Edward Dickinson (father of poetess Emily) made the motion that the town subscribe for $100,000 worth of stock in the Central, providing that its depot be
within a half mile of the center of the town, and that the subscription not be
paid until the full $3,000,000 capitalization was pledged. Dickinson then made
an "earnest and forcible argument in favor of his motion." Local hat manufacturer Henry F. Hills was among other proponents of the subscription. Statis-
tics showing that freight and passenger rates to Boston would be cheaper than
via the current route were cited in the Central's favor.[21]

In spite of these efforts, the meeting turned down Dickinson's motion by a
vote of 228-153.   James M. Stone must have been doubly disappointed to learn
that Hardwick also turned down a subscription in a vote that same week. Amherst's action touched off a wave of ridicule by some of its neighbors, which
was expressed in letters and editorials in area newspapers.

A Northampton letter writer said that people in his town considered Amherst
to be "small potatoes" after the vote. An editorial in the Northampton paper
referred to Amherst's falling into "Rip Van Winkle's sleep." The editor of the
Barre Gazette slyly pointed out that Amherst "greatly benefitted" from state ap-
propriations for its agricultural college, yet the vote showed that the town
lacked "a very strong purpose... to help themselves." A Hadley writer thought
that "the shortsighted men in town meeting... succeeded in cursing their town
for all time."[22]

Whether or not shame had anything to do with it, Amherst friends of the Central arranged to get another vote on the matter held in early October. Several
letters to the *Amherst Record* that September mirrored the local disagreements
over the issue. One letter writer, signing himsewlf "Mechanic," thought that
the opponents of the railroad were the same class of people who were "exceed-
ingly nice in their tastes," and had "sensitive nerves" discouraged new business and industry from coming to the town. A local college professor asked
that Amherst "redeem the deed of haste and ignorance" of the earlier vote.[23]

Opponents of the Central expressed themselves in the newspapers as well.
"Stillwater" thought that the line should not go to Northampton, but northwest

toward the Hoosac Tunnel. He saw the private investors as potentially shutting out the towns, so that "ere long they would own the road." Another writer sarcastically issued a "protest" against "that great through line to the West ... running hither and yon until it reaches the tunnel at Shelburne Falls."[24]

Stone ventured to Amherst at the end of September to hold meetings in the different neighborhoods of town where he "very clearly expounded" the advantages and benefits of the Mass. Central. Constant Southworth of Hardwick met with Stone around this time. He promised Stone that, even though the Swift River valley towns had used up their subscriptions on the Athol & Enfield RR, that he would raise private capital for the Central there.[25]

The Amherst town meeting was held on October 2. Debate on the issue took up two hours; the balloting another two and a half hours. The announcement of the vote as 369-270 in favor of the Central brought "deafening cheers" from proponents. The *Amherst Record* joyfully reported that "boys built a bonfire on the common, and a salute was fired in honor of the occasion." In spite of charges that votes were bought, or the ballot box stuffed, Amherst had subscribed for $100,000 of stock in the Central.[26]

With Amherst's subscription assured, Stone and his fellow directors felt confident enough to take the final action needed to arrange for work on the railroad to begin. In early October, 1870, Norman C. Munson was named general contractor for the Mass. Central. Munson was born in Grafton, Mass., in 1820. After receiving his education in local schools, Munson began his railroad career as a laborer on the Boston & Worcester RR. He moved up to become a section maintenance man for the line. Munson married Lucy Emily Hathaway in Grafton, MA in 1841. Only one of their seven children lived to adulthood.

Munson moved up to the position of construction overseer on the Eastern RR. By 1845, he became a subcontractor on the Fitchburg RR, settling in Shirley, a town along that line. The fine home Munson built there was still standing 150 years later. Munson contributed generously to local churches, a cemetery, and a village hall. He also built several houses and a factory in Shirley.

Munson did contracting work for the the Fitchburg RR, and other lines in New Hampshire, New York, and Maryland. In 1858, he began a seventeen year project for the state of Massachusetts and the city of Boston to fill in that city's Back Bay. To carry out this work, Munson brought in fourteen locomotives, 225 cars, and two steam excavators. The profits from this contract (and other Boston filling projects) made him a millionaire. Munson also built a difficult section of track between Putnam and Willimantic Connecticut for the Boston, Hartford & Erie RR, but the company went bankrupt, owing him over a million dollars.

Norman C. Munson
(Mass. State Library, Spec. Coll.)

When he took on the Mass. Central project, Munson was involved in constructing the Middlesex Central RR in Mass., and the Montpelier and Wells River RR in Vermont. With his experience and connections, Munson was seen as a man who would push the construction of the Mass. Central "forward to a speedy termination."[27]

With Munson hired, President Stone now proceeded to begin agitation for extending the chartered route of the Central into Boston. On October 13, he met with several citizens of Waltham, to discuss the route east from Stony Brook through their town. Those attending the meeting were "unamimous in favor of this project," and promised to support it.[28]

The railroad held a major public meeting at the Mercantile Hall in Boston on October 26, 1870. Stone called the meeting to order, noting that the directors had asked delegates from the various towns along the line of the road to attend so that they might hear of the "progress" made on it to date. He noted that "the enterprise was progressing finely, and it was for them today to decide what further steps shall be taken so that the enterprise shall be commenced soon."[29]

After Stone finished his remarks, A. J. Wright of Boston was chosen temporary chairman, and Ansel Wright, Jr., of Northampton the temporary secretary. A committee of seven was chosen to nominate a list of officers for the meeting. In order to be as inclusive as possible, the list included investors and friends of the line from nine different towns. Included were Thomas Talbot. of Billerica (a future Governor), and Constant Southworth.

After these "officers of the day" were elected, Stone read the report of the Board of Directors. This included the statement that "the chief difficulties of the enterprise have been successfully encountered," and that "the only question is whether the work shall be delayed, or pushed forward immediately." Stone noted that all but $600,000 of the required $3,000,000 of stock had been subscribed for. After stating the "business advantages" of the Central, Stone called for "capitalists and merchants" of Boston to help fill out the needed subscriptions. [30]

This report was referred to a committee to consider. While that was going on, several inspirational speeches for the railroad were made. Francis Parker, a Boston director and Treasurer, stressed the legitimacy of the project, by saying "there will be no stock jobbing, no state aid, no Hartford and Erie management about it."[31]

The committee returned to the meeting with several resolutions. These included congratulations to the directors for their efforts, urgings that Boston investors support the line, and promises to seek subscriptions totalling $322,000 from private investors in towns along the line. These resolutions were adopted unanimously.

A Weston man made a motion that the meeting act upon the matter of having the line's charter amended to gain it an entrance into Boston. He felt that this would not only be good for the railroad, but that he could get his town and some of its citizens to subscribe for stock in it. Stone commented that arrangements to do this were already afoot, to correct "one of the mistakes" of its originators. He also urged that subscriptions be filled out, so that the Central would have more clout in the legislature "with 3,000 men at work upon the line." It was voted that directors petition the legislature for an extension of the route. The meeting concluded on that note.[32]

The *Boston Advertiser* thought that the meeting had been one of "spitited and vigorous character." This newspaper was impressed by the private subscription list, and the line was "earnest" in not seeking "opportunity for speculation." Stone felt it had been "a decided success," and "settled the doubting minds" in towns along the line. He pushed Engineer Frost to complete the surveys east of Amherst, looking into possible routes through Pelham and Shutesbury.[33]

The quest for subscriptions was pushed in early November. At a director's meeting early that month, Francis Brigham, of Hudson, reported that his townsmen oversubscribed their share of the additional subscription asked for. L.J. Dudley, of Northampton, wrote an open letter to urge his neighbors to subscribe for stock. Stone went "lecturing" in Hardwick and Belchertown seeking municipal subscriptions from those towns. His efforts were successful in Hardwick, at a town meeting whose attendence was the "fullest in several years." The town voted, after an "exciting and lengthy debate," to subscribe for $28,200 of shares by a margin of 134-90.[34]

On November 7, the railroad was discussed at a meeting of the Boston Board of Trade. The board acted upon a letter from Central director L.J. Dudley, which cited comments from a number of Northampton area businessmen to prove that shipments by current rail lines were slower and more expensive to there from Boston than from New York. It sought "the considerate attention of the businessmen of Boston" in the Central project, which of course meant buying stock. After some discussion, the letter was referred to the board's transportation committee for consideration, and it was agreed to have it published.[35]

At the end of Novemmber, Stone's speechmaking failed to get Belchertown to vote to take $20,000 worth of stock. Stone wouldn't "let go of [Belchertown] so easy," seeking another vote (and addressing another meeting) on December 10.[36] This failed, as did a third try in January, 1871.

Not only Stone and Dudley, but other "attendant sattelites" were conducting "lecturing tours" for the Central. One editor observed that all this activity, along with "various surveys [must] consume some funds." Stone's $4,000 salary as President of the line was not questioned at this time, but would be in later years.[37]

Probably the most serious question asked at this time was "when the Central Corporation proposes to commence work?"[38] This was not fair to the railroad, in that it had to line up all its subscriptions before it could assess stockholders for funds. However, the line's promoters had been ballyhooing impending construction ever since signing on Munson, so that it is not surprising that people would begin to become anxious.

The year 1871 began with the Central conducting its second annual meeting. This was held at the Central Hotel in Clinton, with about fifty people present. They represented towns and individuals holding $2,504,000 worth of shares. The directors' report boasted of their success in spite of the efforts of "rival interests" to "disintegrate and scatter the elements" of municipal and private support they had received. It estimated a cost of about $3,750,000 to build and equip the line, which was well below the maximum authorized capital of $6,000,000. Stone added his "urgent appeal for additonal subscriptions."[39]

Engineer Frost reported that the field surveys for the line's route were almost completed. Treasurer Francis Parker reported that expenditures during the past year came to $9,771.82. The board of directors chosen were: Stone, Joel Hayden of Williamsburg, L.J. Dudley of Northapmton, Henry Hills of Amherst, J. Edwin Smith, Hiram Wadsworth, and E.B. Shattuck of Barre, B. H. Tripp of Rutand, Charles Cutting of Berlin, George Houghton and Francis Brigham of Hudson, and James Draper of Wayland. Stone, Draper, and Parker were reelected to their respective offices.

Later that month, the first hearing was held on the bill to extend the Mass. Central from its eastern terminus at Stony Brook into Boston. Stone testified on behalf of the line at the legislative committee, where he met opposition

from an officer of the Fitchburg RR and landowners in Cambridge. This was the
opening round of a battle that would drag out for several months.

That same month, various schemes involving the Mass. Central, the Ware River
RR and the dormant Holyoke & Belchertown scheme were aired. Plans included combining parts of these railroads with the projected Palmer & Southbridge RR, in
an attempot to make a shorter through line from Boston to Albany. The Ware
River RR had been built from Palmer to Gilbertville (in Hardwick) by the summer
of 1870.   The New London & Northern RR operated this portion of the line, but
did not lease it until early in 1871. This may have been a move to keep the
Mass. Central from exercising its option of combining with the Ware River, and
to save the New London & Northern from doing any additional construction.

Good news for the line came in early February, with an endorsement from the
Boston Board of Trade. This long-sought action would serve to encourage stock
subscriptions from citizens of that city. The Board resolved that it "heart-
ily commends to the capitalists and merchants of Boston this new line... that
it gives the promise of restoring trade of a district... which... has been diverted elsewhere."[40]

The Central's announcement of its chosen route caused consternation in some
towns, especially Barre. That town had been miffed when the Ware River RR indicated that it would bypass the town center by following the valley of its namesake river.   When the Central decided to follow a parallel route two miles
south of the hilltop town center, agitation began to have a branch built to it.
This culminated in a town meeting on March 6, which passed a resolve to seek
the branch to Barre Center "to largely promote the prosperity of the town."[41]
Several surveys were made that spring, and legislative authorization obtained
to build a branch to accomodate Barre. However, the Central took no action to
construct this branch.

In April, the bill authorizing the line's extension into Boston was working
its way through the legislature. It met with several hostile amendments and
"filibustering" on the part of its opponents, inspired by the Fitchburg RR.[42]
One amendment would have prevented the Central from crossing any part of the
Fitchburg RR; another would have increassed the minimum amount of the subscriptions to a total of $5,000,000 before work could commence. The bill did pass,
enabling the line to easily fill out its stock subscription in Boston. The Central announced that its first assessment on stockholders would be made in early
July.

A new snag hit the Central in June; it was determined that the subscriptions
of Northampton and Hadley were no longer valid, due to a proviso that required
all Central stock subscriptions to be obtained within a year of the votes of
those towns. In spite of this delay, director H.F. Hills of Amherst wrote to
his wife on June 26: "...so anxious am I to have the RR put into operation and
so hopeful are the directors of completing the necessary stock taking at their
adjourned meeting tomorrow."[43]

While the "necessary stock taking" was not finished at that meeting, it must
have been decided to press on with getting Northampton and Hadley to reconfirm
their subscriptions. A long letter was sent to the *Northampton Gazette*, signed
by "D" (L.J. Dudley?) pleading with the towns to rectify their error, with the
line "ready to go to work."[44]   Northampton held a town meeting on July 19,
1871, and voted to reaffrim the subscription 381 to 33. H.F. Hills wrote his
wife from a director's meeting on July 27 that "a good feeling exists... the
Mass. Central RR is to be built."[45]

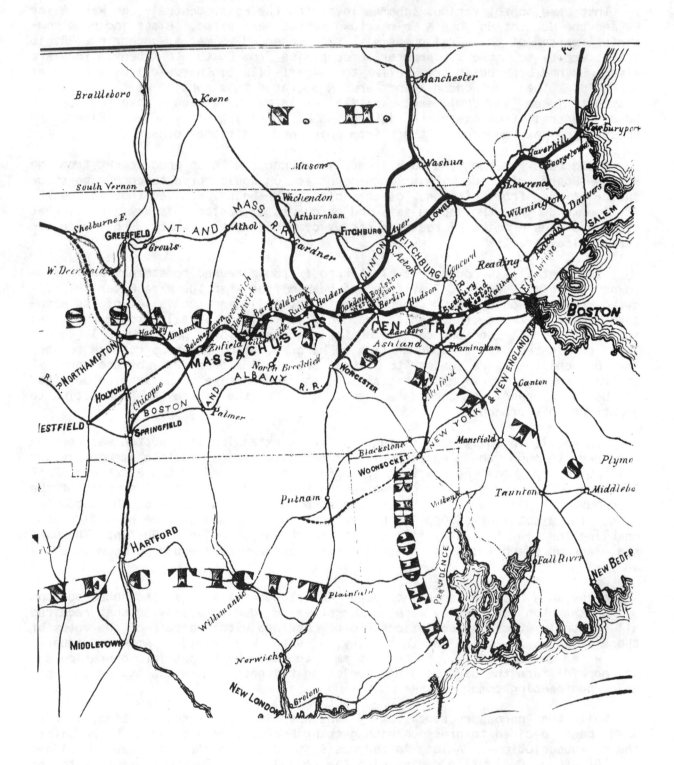

MAP of the MASS. CENTRAL as PROJECTED in 1871
(From 1878 Mass. Central Prospectus)

With the largest municipal subscription set, and the first twenty percent to be paid over, Stone, Frost, and Munson went to Northampton at the beginning of August to arrange for work on the Central's bridge over the Connecticut River. That same day, Northampton's Treasurer S.T. Spaulding questioned the legality of the town's subscription vote, because it included conditions. He got confirmation of his view from two local judges, then refused to pay over the first assessment. Stone and company, upon seeing the "unfriendly disposition manifested there, relinquished their work and returned to Boston."[46]

Hostile newspapers, such as the *Springfield Republican* and a few Boston ones (with help from a "lordly stockholder" of the Fitchburg RR), took advantage of this delay to question the Central's ability to build. Some claimed that signatures on a document signed by the Central's directors were forged. Northampton's Treasurer was accused of having "counsels with enemies of the road," and added to local suspicion by taking an unprecedented vacation on Cape Cod.[47]

In public letters, Stone took his opponents to task for spreading "infamously false" statements about the Central.[48] He obtained a written opinion from a Boston judge upholding Northampton's votes. He also attended a meeting in Northampton at the end of August to assure the citizens of the line's viability. A committee of local residents was appointed at the meeting, headed by L.J. Dudley. After conferring with the town treasurer (back from Cape Cod) and his lawyers, it was decided to hold another town meeting to make a foolproof vote.

The Central's directors met on September 6 to assess the line's situation. The treasurer reported that several towns and many individuals had paid in their assessments before they were due, but the Northampton debacle had caused "all payments to cease." The fact that the Central's charter was up for renewal in the spring of 1872 was cited as a reason for "speedy and decisive action" in getting work on the line underway. It was noted that the intent was still to build to Northampton, so that a connection with the Hoosac Tunnel could be made from there. The directors, in a gesture to bolster the spirits of their Northampton supporters, voted to locate the line through Amherst to that town, providing those town's assessments were paid "without unreasonable delay."[49]

As the time for the town meeting approached, a Northampton newspaper charged that the "big mastiffs" (the Fitchburg and Boston & Albany RR's) were still trying to "plunge their fangs into an innocent victim" (the Central), by knowing "what wires to pull."[50] The fact that both the opposing lines had received state subsidies for their construction was brought out to show how unfair their opposition to a locally-supported line was.

In the town meeting on September 14, Northampton voted overwhelmingly in favor of a legally worded subscription motion, opposing an attempt to delay the vote for three more weeks. With Northampton's assessment finally assured, Stone pushed other towns to pay up. He traveled to Oakham in October to ensure that town's payment. While in that vicinity, he confidently predicted that trains would be running on the Central by December, 1873.[51]

An annual meeting of the Central was held in West Boylston at the beginning of November. The directors reported that "the obstacles which have been with special profuseness thrown in the way of this [compnay] have been substantially overcome or removed." The opposition to the line was called "as unwise as it has been unscrupulous and persistent."[52] All of the stock assessments were paid in, except those of Boylston (was the meeting held near there to spur that town to pay up?) and private shares worth about $10,000. This was expected to be taken up within a week or so.

The election for the board of directors was held, with a nominating committee of one member from each of the towns holding stock, and three at-large members. This committee nominated the current slate, which was unamimously
approved.   After giving "a vote of thanks to the ladies of West Boylston for
their generous and excellent collation," the meeting adjourned.[53]

The Central's board of directors held a meeting in Boston on November 10,
1871.   It voted to sell off the stock subscribed for by the Town of Boylston,
and that of a few individuals, who had not paid in their first assessment.
These subscriptions were taken up by private parties, so that the certifica-
tion of the assessment was filed with the Secretary of State a few days later.
With the first $600,000 of funds made available, Munson was given the okay to
advertise for contracting work on the whole line, and specifically for the
great bridge over the Connecticut River between Northampton and Hadley.

The optimism of Stone and Munson caused them to commit a major error in the
method of constructing the line. Instead of working to complete the line from
the ends toward the middle, they chose to work on the whole route at the same
time.   This prevented them from completing potential income-producing segments
between Amherst and Northampton, and between Sudbury and Boston.   As one newspaper later commented, "the Central tried to do too much, spent its money, and
did nothing."[54]

Munson's "agent" Charles Sweet rented a room over the Savings Bank in Hudson by mid-November. This was to be the field office for the Central, and it
was noted that the room was taken for two years. Stone came into town a few
days later, to scout out a possible location for a depot, but it was decided to
seek input from the townspeople. November 22 was the date set for the subcontractors to examine the section plans for the line to prepare for bidding on
the work. However, Munson failed to appear in his new Hudson office that day,
leaving two dozen contractors high and dry!

With construction about to begin, some of the towns along the route began
to complain about the Central's location. At its November 10 meeting, the board
of directors did not act upon a suggestion by stockholders from Hatfield, Hadley, and Amherst to move the route on their end of the line slightly to the
north.   Hardwick and Barre also expressed concerns about their town centers being left far from the line. This was a great dilemma for the Central, as both
towns had subscribed for stock, and no practical route could be found which
could please both towns at the same time.

Part of the confusion seems to have stemmed from the surveyors coming up with
more than one possible route through several towns, in an attempt to please all
parties involved. As one newspaper commented, "To follow the surveyors of this
central route, is a tedious task. Today they settle on one thing, tomorrow they
reverse it."[55]

The Central's directors had to hold public meetings in two of the towns to
deal with this issue. One was held in Barre, on November 23. Representatives
of the towns of Barre, Petersham, and Hardwick stated the cases for their re-
spective towns. Petersham stood to gain a place on the route if the survey was
run north from Barre Common, then back southward to Hardwick. Constant Southworth, although a director, spoke for Hardwick's interests. The directors ad-
joured the meeting without making a decision.

At a board meeting in early December, it was decided to stay with the original route south of Barre Common and west of Hardwick center, but to offer to
build a branch to the former if Barre would subscribe for an additional $20,000

of stock! A number of people in Barre were not happy with this, one noting
that whan the towns were asked to take stock, they were told that the line
would be built to accomodate the towns on it. But, "when the money was secured, the tactics changed... that the *interest of the road* is everything." A
letter in the *Barre Gazette*, while supporting Barre's interests, pointed out
that the Central had "a varied constituency... and must recognize their duties
to all."[56]

Another well-attended meeting was held in Northampton on December 15, to hear
the route change proposed by parties from Amherst, Hadley, and Hatfield. This
proposal was to put the route north of the proposed line, in order to better
serve Amherst and the northern part of Hadley. Hatfield interests, led by Thad-
deus Graves, contended that moving the site of the bridge over the Connecticut
River to the north would better serve Hatfield. This would induce the town and
several of its residents to subscribe for stock in the Central. Another advantage offered for this route was that it would cross a narrower part of the
river, saving money on the cost of the bridge.

Opponents countered that the new route would put the line a mile and a half
north of the center of Northampton, which could jeopardize that town's stock
subscription.   Captain Enos Parsons led a group of Northampton speakers against
the proposal, and was joined by some from Amherst, led by Edward Dickinson. The
latter group may have felt that any further delay in beginning the work would
be harmful to the Central.

After hearing all of the arguments, some with "considerable spice introduced," the directors adjourned to a dinner. Afterwards, they voted unamimously
not to change the route between Amherst and Northampton, which was "in accord-
ance with the proponderance of public sentiment."[57]

Shortly after the Northampton meeting, Contractor Munson awarded sections
of the line's construction to twenty five different subcontractors. They were
assigned sections from one to ten miles in length, depending on the difficulty
of the terrain. One was from as far away as New Jersey, but most of the labor
would be done by men from Massachusetts. Munson reportedly made his subcontractors agree not to allow any liquor in the work areas, presumably to keep the
workers on an even keel.[58]

Two and a half years after the charter was granted, construction work could
now begin on the Central.

Chapter Three: UNDER CONSTRUCTION

Word of the impending construction work on the Central spread quickly, causing men to flock to towns along the route. Enfield suffered from "an inundation of laborers," many of whom had to be fed and housed by the town.[1] Barracks were built for the workers near Old Furnace in Hardwick. It appears that ground was first broken just after Christmas, 1871. There had been no formal groundbreaking ceremony for the Central, in accord with the wish of the directors. They were quoted as believing that the completion of the line would be the time to celebrate. A ground-breaking ceremony held in Wayland had been merely "an outbreak of local enthusiasm."[2]

As 1872 began, the Central purchased several homes and a slaughterhouse in Northampton to make room for their route. Halfway through the month of January, work was underway in Hardwick, Rutland, Hudson, and Wayland, despite several feet of frost on the ground. The *Boston Advertiser* ran an article about the Central that month, which was reputed to have been "neither written nor solicited by any person connected with the road." It gave a positive review of the Central's prospects, and noted possible extensions of it. These were projected to run to Westfield, via the Belchertown & Holyoke route, or over the old Williamsburg & North Adams route to the Hoosac Tunnel. The article, seeming to ignore the Boston & Albany RR, believed that either of the new routes would "open into Boston the travel and freight of the west."[3]

The Central filed two pieces of legislation for the 1872 session. One was to extend the time for its completion to June 1, 1874. The other, perhaps confirming the *Boston Advertiser*'s suspicions, was to allow the Holyoke & Belchertown RR to combine with the Westfield & Northampton, or the Central. Both of these were passed in the spring, but the Holyoke & Belchertown RR would never progress beyond the point of being surveyed.

Surveyors for the Central were still at work in late January. as one of them was involved in a strange incident in Belchertown. Surveyor Bassett was riding on the New London Northern RR from Amherst to Belchertown, when he jumped off the full speed train at Kelly's Crossing. He hit his head in the fall, and was found unconscious. He was brought to White's Hotel, where a doctor revived him. Bassett had broken no bones, but had been quite badly cut and bruised. A news reporter thought that this "would prove a lesson to him, although he says he has often done it before!"[4]

By the beginning of February, work began on the segment of the line above the Hardwick village of Gilbertville. Ground was broken in Enfield on the 23rd. Noting the circuitous route the Central was to take through West Hardwick toward Enfield, one newspaper wondered why the line wasn't being built through Ware, which would provide more traffic. Another thought that "making an ox bow of eleven miles to get over five is neither profitable nor advantageous."[5] Ironically some of the work done above Gilbertville survives today as parts of High and Upper Church Streets in that village.

These scattered portions of work were draining the Central's limited funds, so it announced that the payment of the second twenty percent assessment on the stock was due by March 1. A circular accompanying this request stated that the Central's "affairs were highly prosperous." This was criticized by one newspaper (from a Boston & Albany town) as being "a comforting assurance" to the towns trying to raise the money. It asked when Stone or Munson "will rise to explain" what became of the money already spent on the road. It concluded, "For ways that are decidedly dark, railroad builders are sometimes peculiar."[6]

The assessment did cause a few grumbles from towns who were dissatisfied with the location of the route. Amherst parties felt that their anxiety over the route would be resolved by witholding their assessment. The town treasurer agreed, and paid over only the interest on it. In spite of this uncertainty, it was reported that "Irishmen" were streaming into Amherst in search of work on the Central.[7]

Some distrust of the Central was expressed at a few of the town meetings held along the line that spring. An attempt was made in Hardwick to require the Selectmen to get town meeting permission to make payments on the stock, but this was defeated. West Boylston instructed their Selectmen to "use all legal measures to defend the rights of the town at any crossing" of a road by the Central, and to make a detailed report of "all the money paid out and expended" in connection with the town's subscription.[8]

Almost all of the towns paid the assessments rapidly, so that by the middle of March, there were over 500 men, and 400 teams of horses working on various segments of the line. The basic construction method to create the necessary cuts and fills for the railbed was labor-intensive. Men shoveled the dirt into horsedrawn carts, then hauled it off to the proper site for dumping. In "one or two instances," a horsedrawn "portable railway" was used to convey earth. Ledges and other rocky obstructions would be blasted away with black powder. One overseer was badly hurt in mid-March by a delayed blast on the line in Enfield.[9]

Use of portable rails and horse-drawn dumpcarts for cuts and fills.
(Chicago Railway Review, Sept. 6, 1873)

President Stone, Contractor Munson, and agents such as Capt. Enos Parsons (a Northampton attorney) made a number of land purchases for the Central, beginning in March. A depot lot was purchased in Enfield for about $1,400. Sometimes the value of a parcel needed by the railroad was inflated wildly by its owner. In one instance near Enfield, the landowner countered the railroad's offer of $25 with a figure of $1,000 for a strip of land. These disputes were often settled by the County Commissioners, but a few ended up in court.

The arrival of warm weather in April made many of the subcontractors "jubilant" about pushing the work. Munson himself took time off from his Boston filling project to make a tour of the whole route. Perhaps due to his tour, a section of the route in Enfield was relocated, reducing the length of the route by "nearly a mile." Munson expressed confidence that the line would be "in running condition within two years."[10] One Enfield man must have been pleased at the extra work in that town; David Blodgett opened up a granite quarry to supply the contractors.

One of the more difficult sections on the Central route was in West Rutland. A large cut had to be made to get through Charnock (or Shannock) Hill. It was estimated that 60,000 yeards of fill would have to be removed for the cut. Just west of that point, a high fill would have to be made to get across Long Pond. A handbill was circulated, seeking a hundred men to work in this section, for a wage of $1.75 per day. Curiously, the handbill was not issued under the name of the railroad, or Contractor Munson, but by "J.M. Stone & Co."[11] The subcontractor for the section west of these obstacles was H. Sherwood, from Ontario, Canada.

Work on the Central came to a halt in West Boylston on May 8, when workers went on strike for more pay. This was quickly settled, but it would not be the last time a strike slowed work on the Central. Conditions were not easy for the laborers, who worked long hours, and sometimes had to wait weeks for their pay. Munson's prohibition of liquor at the worksites and barracks did not prevent the men from seeking solace in the nearby villages.

Gilbertville seemed to be especially afflicted with problems caused by railroad workers. One report maintained that "bodily and spiritual needs are provided for, and criminals tried under one roof" there. When Constable Dexter became "active in his opposition to the liquor traffic" in that village, threats were made on his life, and one of his cows was shot dead. At this time, it was noted that Gilbertville was "infested with a miserable gang of roughs, who constitute a portion of the help employed by the Mass. Central."[12]

The month of June, 1872 saw its ups and downs for the Central. The Town of Barre was still not satisfied with the Central's route through town, and held a public meeting to resolve the matter. The "large number present" chose a committee of three men to "consult with the directors of the road" on Barre's behalf. The directors apparently did not wish to change their stance that the town would have a branch only if were willing to pay extra for it.[13]

That month, the Central expressed an interest in the extension of the Athol & Enfield RR. This line, which had been built in 1871 to connect Athol and the New London & Northern RR at Barrett's Junction, ran parallel to the Central's route in Greenwich and Enfield. The Athol & Enfield got legislative approval to extend from Barrett's to Springfield, as the Springfield, Athol, & NE. RR. The extension now made this previously local route potentially valuable to both the Central and the New London & Northern (which had been leased by Vermont Central RR interests in 1871). However, the Springfield, Athol, & NE. RR was able to raise the necessary funds to complete the extension, so it did not return either suitor's interest in it.

Also in June, the Central and the towns on the western end of the line received good news, with the awarding of the contract for the bridge over the Connecticut River. The subcontractor was John R. Smith, of Springfield. The price for the 1400 foot long structure was $140,000. As it later became known, the contract was awarded under unusual circumstances, which would be brought out during a legislative committee investigation.

The bid process for the bridge contract started out with a standard advertisement in late 1871. Munson recalled later that he had received "six or eight
bids," ranging in price from $135,000 to $155,000.[14] One of the bidders was
John R. Smith, who was affiliated with A.D. Briggs, a noted bridge builder and
a member of the Mass. Board of Railroad Commissioners.

Another potential bidder, R.F. Hawkins, a well-known Springfield bridge
builder, stated that when he did not receive an invitation to bid on the bridge
contract, he wrote to Munson, but received no reply. Upon hearing that "Briggs
was going for it pretty strong, and the Northampton competition was going for
it pretty strong," he felt it was "no use" for him to put in a bid.[15]

Who was this "Northampton competition?" A previously unkown combination of Julius S. Hartwell, E. D.
Wells, and Gen. Luke Lyman, all from
Northampton. Hartwell was a general
contractor,and had worked with Wells
before. Lyman, an "intimate friend"
of Hartwell's, was very influential
in town, being Register of Probate
for Hampshire County. Lyman had
served as the moderator of the two
town meetings which had reaffirmed
Northampton's subscription to the
Central, and was a member of the
town's committee to oversee the assessment payments. Lyman later admitted that he had "no previous ex-

Luke Lyman

perience with bridges," and that he had gotten into the scheme "to make money." A lawyer for A.D. Briggs later called this a "fancy bid, by a fancy firm,"
with "insufficient specifications" to do the job correctly.[16]

Hartwell got their bid in on May 7. He later testifed that when he handed
in the bid, Mr. Warner, Munson's clerk, told him that their bid was the lowest.
Three weeks went by; Munson later claimed he was sick at home during that
time. On May 30, 1872, Munson telegraphed Hartwell and Lyman to see him in his
Boston office. When they arrived at Munson's office the next day, according to
Hartwell, Munson told them that "there was another bid substantially the same"
as theirs, and that it "was important to give it to the other parties." Lyman
recalled that "Munson expressed himself as though it was for his interest that
we should retire."[17]

Munson later recalled that when he told Hartwell and Lyman "that he would a-
ward the contract to another," they "became rather excercised over it." Hartwell stated that Munson told them that "he would make us satified, if they
would relinquish their claim." Munson testified that he felt that he had "com-
mitted myself to them enough to have given them a claim against me." They negotiated over this for "two or three hours," according to Munson, when he asked
them "if they would take a certain amount, and throw up their contract." They
asked for the sum of $12,000, which they figured would have been their profit
on the contract. Munson thought that figure was "rather high," and made a
counter offer of $2,000.[18]

They finally settled upon a figure of $6,000, which Munson gave to Hartwell
in the form of a personal note, due within six months. Hartwell received his
money when the note was due, and split it equally with his two partners, who
were "fully satisfied to take what we could get."[19]

Munson's use of a six month note would seem to confirm his later testimony that he paid off the Northampton men for their "goodwill... so that "they would not work against the road." Munson added that he thought "they had been influential" in obtaining Northampton's stock subscription," although both Lyman and Hartwell said they had only voted for it as individuals. Munson testified he had paid them "on his own judgement," and defended this method of guaranteeing municipal subscriptions, by a euphemism; "we had to manage these things a little." Stone denied any "knowledge about the contract," having left all of the details to Munson.[20]

The other possible reason for Munson to award the bridge contract to John Smith would have been to curry favor with the latter's partner, Mass. Railroad Commissioner Briggs. Smith and Briggs both claimed that Smith had made the bid on his own, and not for the firm they both belonged to. Munson testified thet he thought Smith "was the proper man" to carry out the contract, and that Hartwell & Co.'s. bid specifications were "not satisfactory." Munson asserted that the fact that Smith's business partner was Briggs did not have "one particle of influence" on his awarding the bid.[21]

There is no evidence that Munson ever gained anything from Briggs by this gesture. However, another investigation that same year showed that Munson had been involved in a scheme with a state director of the Boston & Albany RR on a gravel hauling contract in Boston. While "no favor was shown to Munson" in the process, the state director was able to rake off a substantial profit for himself.[22]

The whole sad bridge episode may have been merely a case of buying influence. When it was aired in public in 1876, it reflected poorly on most of the people involved. It also raises the question of whether Munson used Central funds for the "payoff" to Hartwell & Co. If he did, did he also misappropriate other money from the railroad, thus causing overspending to take place?

The arrival of summer in 1872 found work in full swing along the route of the Central. It was reported that work was being done at thirty places between Weston and Northampton. Surveys were being made to determine what route would be best for the line to enter Boston. Injuries continued to occur in the work: a laborer in the western part of Belchertown was bruised and suffered a broken leg when a sand bank caved in on him, and an "Irishman" was killed by a premature powder blast in West Boylaton. Contractor Foley, working near Gilbertville, was severely injured by a powder blast in September, causing a rumor that work had shut down on his section.

The work was also causing landowners to petition their County Commissioners to settle their land claims with the railroad. Hiram Tucker, of Hardwick, had his hearing with the Worcester County Commissioners in late June. His 70 acre farm was bisected by the Central, which had offered him $400 for a settlement. The Commissioners adjourned to consider the matter, as they also had to settle claims in West Boylston and Berlin that summer. Hampshire County Commissioners were also kept busy hearing several claims in Enfield later that summer.

A third assessment on the stockholders, due in August, was called to pay for the work contemplated in the autumn. The Central was trying to firm up its route into Boston by arranging with the Boston & Lowell RR to join its tracks with the Lexington Branch. This seemed to be the Central's only choice, since the Fitchburg RR, the other potential connection, was hostile to it.

Problems with liquor consumption by Central workmen continued to vex local authorities along the line. A raid was conducted at a Greenwich establishment in August, which confiscated some liquors. A "shanty" on the line in the same town, run by "a Frenchman" was also raided, where "implements of the rum traffic," but no liquor were seized. This did not stop "noisy gangs of foreigners" from "getting drunk and hooting at passersby" in Greenwich and Hardwick a few weeks later.[23]

In Clinton, several seizures of liquor took place in September. An unofficial, but most amusing "seizure" took place on Wilson Hill. It seems that some Central laborers learned of a woman in that vicinity who had obtained a ten gallon keg of whiskey. To gain posession of it for themselves, one of them called upon the lady, and "read extracts from a newspaper to her," while the others stole the keg from her house. The men hid the liquor in the woods, later indulging in "a most glorious free drink."[24]

Drinking was not the only problem with laborers on the line. A pay cut, from $2.00 to $1.75 a day, was announced on the eastern part of the line in early October. This caused several strikes of the laborers. A number of the strikers were let go, and "men brought in from Boston" to replace them within a couple of weeks.[25]

Laborers were not the only problem element in the construction of the line. Contractors Cook and Lansing, working around Hudson, reportedly found that the job "would not pay." They absconded in late August, after receiving a payment from Munson, leaving workers and local suppliers unpaid. Since they were from New Jersey, they eluded efforts to locate them, so the equipment they left behind was auctioned off a couple of months later. Munson annulled their contract, and reissued it to other parties, so that work could resume.[26]

Work on the bridge over the Connecticut River at Northampton was slowed by shifting sand at the foundation of one of the piers on the west side. Eventually, piles had to be driven 115 feet before bedrock was hit. By year's end, the abutments on both sides of the river were completed, as was the first pier on the west side. When the river froze over after New Year's, the work horses were able to cross over it on the ice.

Land settlements continued to cost the Central money. In late September, the Worcester County Commissioners granted Hardwick farmer Hiram Tucker $1,059 and costs for the bisection of his property by the Central, but he took his case to court to seek a higher amount. Benjamin Ward of Enfield was awarded $1,800 by the Hampshire County Commissioners.

The Central filed its annual report with the Massachusetts Railroad Commission as of the end of September. It noted that $894,080 had been paid in on the $3,000,000 in stock. Direct construction expenses had already equalled this at $891,020, with land damages adding another $112,884.29. Engineering and salary expenses added up to $78,554. With interest costs included, the Central had expended a little over a million dollars, causing it to be running a deficit of $202,686. This was presumably done in anticipation of obtaining the unpaid assessments, plus the fourth one, which was due on December 1.

In October, the Central directors voted to locate the line on the south side of the Ware River in Barre, which was done to avoid building at least two bridges over that river. This action put the line even further away from the town's center that the original layout, so it caused much indignation there. Amherst's witholding of its subscription moneys until the route of the line was firmly established there was cited as an example for Barre to emulate.

One letter to the *Barre Gazette* pointed out that even if a branch line to the town center were built by the Central, the promised connection with Worcester through Holden would be at a separate grade, thus being inconvenient. This writer criticized the Central for having "misled and misused" Barre by "the most successful job of wool-pulling in regard to the subscription money that I ever heard of." He bemoaned "what a heavy horse we've been riding for the past two or three years, and the diminutive donkey we are astride now."[27]

Knowing that the Central's third annual meeting was approaching, Stone tried to smooth over the hard feelings in Amherst about the line's route, and rebut newspaper criticism. In a letter to a Northampton newspaper, Stone asserted that "A remarkable fertility of invention has been displayed in making statements about the Mass. Central RR. These misrepresentations it has generally been thought to let pass as 'idle wind.'" He blamed the Amherst problem on local requests to resurvey the route, and on the town's difficulty to borrow the necesary funds to meet its assessments.[28]

The editor of the *Amherst Record* thought that only a few people did not believe that the Central's route would meet the terms of the subscription. However, he did express a lack of "patience with somebody or another for not making some show of commencing the work," or even negotiating for "a foot of land" in Amherst. This might have struck a chord with Stone, for surveyors were sent into Amherst in November, and a Central office opened there before year's end.[29]

Stone did not make the right moves for Hardwick, as that town held a special town meeting on its Central subscription on November 5. Since the Central had been grading on the New Braintree side of the Ware River, it appeared that Furnace village would not get a depot conveniently located for it. The town meeting voted to withhold the remaining sixty percent of the stock assessment until "the depot in the vicinity of the Old Furnace Village be located within the limits of the Town of Hardwick."[30] Even though the Central had accomodated Hardwick with the circuitous route through the western part of town, this latest change negated the goodwill that route had engendered.

Just before the Central's annual meeting, it was noted that work in Sudbury was "being vigorously prosecuted," especially a ledge cut. An amusing scare headline apperared in a Greenfield newspaper at that time. This viewed the Central as trying to "fix" the legislature to give them a route to the Hoosac Tunnel, then nearing completion. This scheme would see either the Williamsburg & North Adams proposal, or a new connection from Northampton to the Troy & Greenfield RR at Conway used to "divert" the tunnel's traffic to the Central, and away from the intended Fitchburg RR (and Greenfield). The *Barre Gazette* reproduced this "Mare's Nest" for the amusement of its readers.[31] While there was agitation for a line northwest out of Northampton, the intent appears to have been to connect that town (and/or the Central) with the tunnel, rather than to monopolize it.

The third annual meeting of the Mass. Central was held at the Hudson Town Hall on November 5. After the financial report was read, Engineer Frost reported that sixty of the ninety two sections of the line were currently being worked upon, all east of Belchertown. He noted that close to forty miles of the grade was prepared for ballasting and track, and that Munson had "wisely" caused many culverts and small bridges to be built ahead of the grading. The delays in sinking part of the foundation of the Northampton bridge was noted, but Frost optimistically felt that a "cosiderable portion of the truss superstructure would be in place" by the end of the following year.[32]

Stone than read the directors' report, which expressed the hope that the next annual meeting would be held in Boston, as that would then be a town "on the line of the railroad." The directors congratulated themselves on their "promptness" in settling land claims, and lauded the "efficiency and good management" of Munson as contractor.[33]

The old board of directors was re-elected; they, in turn, re-elected Stone as President and Draper as Clerk. The stockholders present voted to authorize the directors to arrange for terminal facilities in Boston with another line, and to issue bonds to help pay for the completion of the construction. Stone noted that negotiations for an entrance into Boston were being carried out, and that "if all signs did not fail, the cars of the [Central] would be running into Boston in less than six months." This would not cost the Central "millions of dollars" to achieve, as some detractors had asserted.[34]

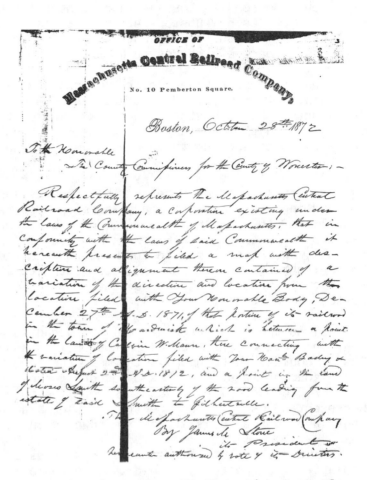

Letter from James M. Stone (on Central letterhead) to Worcester County Commissioners, which accompanied filing of layout of Central's route in that county.
(Worcester County Commisioners)

As 1872 came to a close, there were many proposals flying about for new lines to connect with the Central. One was another version of the line running west out of Worcester, surveyed through Leicester and North Brookfield. This would strike the Central in Hardwick, follow it to the Springfield, Athol, & NE RR, and form a quicker route to Springfield than the Boston & Albany RR. The other proposed line was to run east from Worcester to the Central at Berlin, for an alternate route to Boaton. While neither of these proposals came to pass, they show that the Central was highly regarded in some quarters as a potential connector for alternative routes to the Boston & Albany RR.

The Central scored a coup by coming to an arrangement with the Boston & Lowell RR to use the latter's facilities in Boston. As the Boston & Lowell was building a new station and terminal on the north side of Boston, this would provide the Central with first class passenger and freight facilities. Central trains would use the Boston & Lowell's Lexington Branch to reach Boston. This meant that the Central would have to survey a route from Stony Brook to meet the Lexington Branch somewhere in Cambridge.

Why did the Boston & Lowell agree to this arrangement with a partially-built line? It appears that the Boston & Lowell had been blocked by the New Hampshire legislature from attempting to expand its system in that state. This left the Boston & Lowell with a need for new feeder lines, especially with freight for its new Boston terminal. Since the Central was tapping a long strip of territory with no direct link to Boston, it appears to have been a shrewd move on the part of the Boston & Lowell.[35]

The same Boston newspaper that had analyzed the Central's prospects at the beginning of the year did so again at the end. It was very positive about the agreement with the Boston & Lowell RR. While it noted the many gaps in the grading work on the Central, it optimistically stated that the line would be "open and working between Boston and Northampton by next Christmas Day."[36]

1873 would be a "peak" year in the life of the Central, with its prospects in January looking much better than the results at year's end. The major issue confronting the line as the year began were two proposals involving the Hoosac Tunnel. Both of these were filed as bills before the state legislature. One was to allow the Boston & Lowell RR to consolidate with the Fitchburg, and presumably, with the lines to the west through the tunnel. The other was to allow the Fitchburg RR to consolidate with its satellites east of the tunnel, the Vermont & Massachusetts and the Troy and Greenfield RRs, and with the Troy & Boston RR, west of the tunnel.

Since the Mass. Central still harbored some hopes of putting through an extension toward the tunnel, these bills caused its directors to be concerned. They "could see no good in the movement" of "the railroad monopolists" to pass consolidation measures. The directors got petitions out in towns along the Central route opposing consolidation. These were forwarded to the legislature. Representatives of the Central would make their feelings known both at hearings, and to the legislators from towns along the route.[37]

The agitation about the tunnel did focus the Central's attention on two possible routes their line could take to approach it. One route was the long dormant one northwest from Northampton. This underwent a temporary revival in early 1873. A time extension for a line northwest from Williamsburg had been granted by the legislature. A group formed under the name of the Northampton & Shelburne Falls RR, with a view that this route was superior in grade to the route of the old Williamsburg & North Adams RR. They met in Conway at the end of January, electing Central director Joel Hayden President. They voted to seek stock subscriptions, or to negotiate with the Central to build their line. Unfortunately, this proposal never got off the ground, either due to a lack of local money, or the inability of the Central to exploit it.

Even if the Central couldn't find a way to go directly toward the tunnel from Northampton, it could attempt to do so from Amherst. In late February, it was reported that a survey "in a very direct line" had been made from Amherst to a point west of Greenfield, to connect with the Troy & Greenfield RR. The reporter opined that "it is probable that a road over this route will sometime be built." This story caused much consternation in Northampton, which feared that the Central would leave it on a mere branch line. Enos Parsons, the Central's Northampton agent, addressed a letter to President Stone on this subject in early March.[38]

Stone replied that the Central had "nothing to do with" a line northwest of Amherst, only " a railroad from Stony Brook... to Northampton." He sarcasticly observed that since Nothampton and Amherst people had "insisted that our line should run to Amherst Centre... so far northward toward Deerfield, it is not strange that Amherst people should turn their eyes in the direction of the tunnel line at Deerfield?" Stone placed the blame for the new survey on "Amherst people," when Norman Munson was actually the one responsible for it, possibly with Stone's approval.[39]

Stone asserted "that I have done all that I could to keep attention... turned to the Northampton & Shelburne Falls as our line to the tunnel." He saw the proposed Deerfield route as "feasible," but "costly," due to two large bridges that would have to be built. While admitting that this route could be a profitable "feeder" for the Central, Stone stated that his "influence" would be used to "bring western business on to our line at Northampton, and thus utilize a lerger portion of our own line."[40]

Whatever the possibilities for branches or extensions, the work on the existing route was continuing. To pay for this, stockholders were instructed to pay their fifth assessment by March 7. Some of the towns still held back due to local dissatisfaction with the route. It was "hinted" to Wayland that if it did not pay up, its stock would be sold, and it would still be liable for the assessments.[41] Still, there were sufficient funds to continue the work on the grading, and the Northampton bridge through the summer.

In the spring, Stone and some of the directors visited the site of the large fill near West Rutland. They were expecting to bring in steam derricks and drills for work on the cut near there. They also reviewed some of the grade crossings along the line, as both the Hampshire and Worcester County Commissioners met to consider these at that time.

It is not known whether Stone or his cohorts took notice of several letters that appeared in the *Barre Gazette* that spring. One of them bemoaned the fact that Barre had nothing to show for its investment in the Central, not even "a shovel put into the earth," which was true. Another felt that "Barre mistook its enemies for its friends" when it voted for Central stock. A third writer called the Central "a corporation with no soul and an empty pocket."[42] Barre's grumbles were matched by Waltham's, where townspeople couldn't agree on which of two possible Central routes through town they preferred. Many disliked the numerous grade crossings on one route, while property owners opposed the other one.

While the Central was continuing its construction, the legislative committee studying the Hoosac Tunnel consolidation bills issued two reports. The majority report recommended a consolidation of the Fitchburg RR, the two lines leading to the tunnel from it, and the Troy & Boston RR. A minority report sought to have the state own this system of railroads. L.J. Dudley spoke at a hearing on these proposals on behalf of the Central. He advocated keeping the tunnel open to all traffic, between the state line on the west and Greenfield to the east. Dudley hoped that the "Central would not be ignored just because the road is not done." The Fitchburg RR managed to have both of the bills defeated, but this would not be the last of the consolidation issue.[43]

Other railroads were still considering the Central to be a potential partner in regional schemes. The proposal for a line west of Worcester, through the Brookfields, to the Central in Hardwick was the subject of a meeting in Spencer in late May. This was attended by officials and "capitalists" from several towns, including Worcester. Another, more enticing connector to the Central was proposed to run from Southbridge toward Greenfield. This would utilize either a part of the existing Central route near Enfield, or the proposed extension northwest of Amherst. It was seen as a connector to Providence, RI. While a railroad between Palmer and Southbridge would be attempted four decades later, nothing came of this at the time.

Fatal accidents continued to occur on the construction of the Central, some with sad results. A man was killed by a derrick falling on him in Rutland in April. Contractor Sherwood believed that it was the first time a man in his employ had died in his four decades of railroad building. A "Nova Scotia" man was also killed by a falling derrick in Greenwich a few weeks later. Laborers Michael Brady (who had a wife and eight children) and Michael Dwyer were killed north of Gilbertville in late August. A banking collapsed on them, crushing them both. Contractor Foley stated that these were the first men in his employ to be killed in his seventeen years of working on railroads. Another Irishman, Dennis Murphy, died as a result of "carelessness" when he caused a banking to cave in at West Rutland in September.[44]

Problems with laborers' off the job activities continued as well. After a pay day in Oakdale in the early spring, "work was given up," when the laborers found out that there was a local rumseller. Many of the laborers went on "a general drunk as a consequence." Two state constables investigated to find the source of the rum. After a "search which led through numerous trap doors, and intricate windings," two brothers were arested for illegal rum selling.[45] A laborer in Rutland one night several months later "imbibed a little too freely." He passed out in a gutter, and died from exposure the next day."[46]

A more amusing incidence of drunkenness involved two "Irishmen" who were working on the Central in Greenwich. At the end of one work day early in the summer, these two took the S.A. & NE RR train to Palmer. There they "filled up with whiskey," and took the evening train back towards Greenwich. The conductor threw them off the train in Enfield, where Sheriff Potter relieved each of them of a bottle of whiskey. After "raving and threatening for awhile, one of them started on the track for Greenwich, with a great pressure of steam." When he reached the bridge over the Swift River, he "lost his balance," and fell into the river. Two men, who were working on a nearby church fished him out of the water. The drunk reportedly "knew but very little of what had happened until the next morning. The other Irishman spent the night in jail. Both had to pay a twelve dollar fine before being released.[47]

Raising enough money to finish the constrcution of the Central seemed to be a problem as the summer of 1873 came to a close. The last stock assessment was called for in September, to be paid by October 15. According to their annual report to the state, as of September 30, 1873, the Central had only received $1,727,229 in payments on their stock, while expenses had reached $2,569,333. This was made up by issuing $995,000 of first mortgage bonds, which were given to Munson to pay for work.

In order to raise the necessary funds, It was decided to try to market more bonds overseas. Hugh McCulloch, a former Secretary of the U. S. Treasury, was retained to market Mass. Central bonds in England. In mid-September, McCulloch had negotiated an agreement with a British banking house to handle $2,700,000 of these bonds, which would have been enough to finish and equip the road.[48]

Unfortunately for the Central, and many other corporate fundraisers at that time, the Philadelphia banking house of Jay Cooke closed its doors. Cooke had made a fortune marketing bonds for the government during the Civil War. Afterwards, he got into promoting securities for many enterprises, especially railroads. Cooke invested heavily in the Northern Pacific RR, which was then under construction. Due to huge outlays for labor and equipment (genuine and dishonest), the project's debt was $7,000,000 ahead of funds. To stave off disaster, Cooke bought many of the railroad's bonds himself. The uncertain situation made many of Cooke's depositors seek to withdraw their funds from his banks.

President U.S. Grant visited Cooke at his palatial home in a Philadelphia suburb on September 17. The next morning, Cooke was telegraphed that demands exceeded deposits at his New York branch, so it was closed. Cooke hurried into his Philadelphia office, saw the game was up, and closed it at noon. This action had an immediate effect on the money markets in the whole United States, setting off what historian Dee Brown called "the most percipitant and widespread economic disaster since the birth of the republic."[49]

According to a later statement by L.J. Dudley, news of Cooke's failure was telegraphed to London that evening. Since "many millions of his bonds had been fearlessly purchased there... his failure paralyzed confidence in American railroad securities." That caused the British bankers to refuse to carry out the agreement with McCulloch, which was to have been signed that day.[50]

This was later known as the Panic of 1873, and it was the beginning of an economic depression that lasted several years. As Dudley succinctly put it, the "financial trouble... put an end to railroad building in this country, made bankrupt a multitude of roads already built, suspended dividends on a multitude more, and paralyzed the other corporate and business enterprises of the country." This explains one of the major reasons why the Mass. Central would soon slip into a limbo that was to last for most of the rest of the decade.[51]

Chapter Four: **IN LIMBO**

The panic of 1873 had a serious effect on Norman Munson, among others. He was owed $1,300,000 for contracting work when the Boston, Hartford & Erie RR went bankrupt in 1870. Munson was also involved in at least two other railroads at the time, and he had done some "unfortunate land speculation." On top of all this, Munson had taken much of his pay for the Central work in bonds, and had only paid in forty percent of the cost of the $1,933,000 in Central stock he had taken. The prospect of Munson's "failure" was admitted at the Central's annual meeting a few weeks later.[1]

Work continued on some parts of the Central route for several weeks after the panic. About half of the grading and culverting was finished, and over two thirds of the right of way secured when the money ran out around November 1. Work in Greenwich, Hardwick and Rutland came to a halt as contractors laid off their crews. Laborers in the first two places were not paid for their last two or three months on the job. This was definitly a hardship for most of the men, a few of whom were owed as much $400. Some of them hired a lawyer to press their claims. One case made it as far as the state Superior Court, but was denied because they tried to collect the money from the railroad, not the subcontractor.

One newspaper commented that this was "not the first time such transactions have been practiced in this neighborhood." It ruefully concluded that "If our resources cannot be developed without cheating every laborer who works on the road, every man who subscribes, every town through which a railroad passes, and oftentimes the state, then it is high time that railroads should be put on the same basis with all other enterprises."[2]

These defaults were not mentioned at the company's fourth annual meeting in early November. This was held in Hudson Town Hall, with Stone presiding. Engineer Frost gave a glowing report of the accomplishments to that date, noting that the work had been "pushed with vigor and success." He painted a rosy picture of the future connections "with the coal fields and mines of New York and Pennsylvania, the commerce of the lakes, the forests of Canada, and the grainfields of the Northwest." Frost also pointed out that there was only three months work left to do on the Northampton bridge, and a few months of grading between there and Enfield.[3]

The treasurer's report was read; it was admitted that the British bond deal had fallen through because of the panic. Only three towns had not paid their full subscriptions; most of the unpaid funds were from individual stockholders. Director Francis Brigham lauded the board of directors for having "done all that it was possible for them to do to forward the enterprise." He stated his belief that it was "hard for all new railroads to move fast under the present financial difficulty."[4] Franklin Bonney, of Hadley, was elected to fill Joel Hayden's place on the board of directors; the others were re-elected.

Stone reassured the shareholders that the Central "would be built and equipped for the amount of the contract with Mr. Munson." As the time promised for the completion of the road had passed, the question was asked when the line would be open from Hudson to Boston. The reply was given to be "within twelve months." A Mr. Joslin urged that the Central should lose no time "to push forward the project of building the road from Amherst to the Hoosac Tunnel." He also urged that the Central lay rail on the eastern end of the route to put it "in operation for earning money as soon as possible."[5] If this advice had been taken in 1873, the Central might have weathered the ensuing inancial depression much better than it did.

While the Central could be optimistic at its annual meeting, the cessation of work, suits by unpaid laborers, and "various damaging reports of an exhausted treasury" caused many of the line's old enemies to "croak, I told you so!" Reports of these views were conveyed to Stone by Enos Parsons in a letter late in December. Stone replied with "cheering words" that "the doubts and fears of all of our Northampton friends will be happily resolved in due time." He thought that they would be "fools" to "smash ahead and sacrifice our resources... We don't propose to do this, we prefer to husband our resources and let our friends despond for the present, and rejoice by and by." At the end of his letter to Parsons, Stone expressed final judgement on the prospects of the Central: "There is no doubt about the railroad being completed."[6]

One prominant Northampton citizen wasn't buying any of this. Charles Delano replied to Stone's letter a week later with a biting attack on the railroad as one of the main causes of Northampton's high tax rate. Delano asserted that if Northampton had gone along with the construction of the proposed branch line to Amherst, they would have had it "running in 1872." But instead, he felt, Stone had "beguiled" the voters into supporting a "Grand through route" instead. Delano regarded Stone's latest message as typical of his readiness to "furnish 'cheering words' to order, when the people began to be clamorous over his unredeemed pledges." He ridiculed Stone's "husbanding our resources" comment by asking, "what resources have they to husband?"[7]

The newspaper's editor, who received his own share of Delano's barbs, considered the writer's attacks as "mere personal flings and sneers." The editor thought that Delano was trying to divert the attention of the townspeople from other local probelms by focusing upon the Central. However, the editor did not choose to answer most of Delano's telling points, perhaps because he knew that "cheering words" alone would not suffice.[8]

1874 opened with the Boston & Albany RR stealing a march on the Central. This was done when the Boston & Albany ratified a lease of the Ware River RR in January. The Ware River, which the Central had been authorized to combine with, had not been completed north of the Palmer to Gilbertville segment. The route of this line between Gilbertville and Barre paralleled the Central for about ten miles. The Ware River was operated by the New London & Northern RR under a lease agreement.

Ginery Twichell, a director of the Boston & Albany, was a former stage driver through Barre, and a principal in the Boston, Barre & Gardner RR. In 1872, He suggested to his fellow directors that it might be prudent for their line to gain control of the Ware River, to prevent it from "coming together" with the Central and "forming a connecting line." Such a combination would have "caused an injury" to the B&A, by draining off business from the Barre and Hardwick area.[9] Twichell saw the Central's potential as a rival to their line as a "terrible reality." He also saw potential for a connection between the Ware River RR in Barre and the Boston, Barre & Gardner RR in Princeton.[10]

Other directors of the Boston & Albany seemed to agree with Twichell's fears of competition from the Central - Ware River combination. E.B. Gillett thought that the Ware River "had capacity of much mischief and loss to the Boston & Albany if it passed into other hands." He thought that the Central could combine with the Ware River, and the Springfield, Athol, & NE to create an alternative route from Springfield to Boston.[11]

Boston & Albany Vice-President D.W. Lincoln later published a statement admitting that the "Central... was threatening to become a formidable competitor for our business, local as well as through, and every outside influence was in its favor." He felt that if the Central "was constructed and in alliance with [the Ware River], it would have diverted the whole eastern business of the Ware River valley from our road."[12]   Lincoln also testified that he didn't understand the Central to be "defunct at all," and that "they didn't cease to be a competitor for business."[13]

Isaac Ross, a state appointed director of the Boston & Albany, (and Superintendent of the Boston, Barre & Gardner RR), stated that it was expressed at a board meeting that "the fear was that [the Central], striking down into that valley, might take away some of this business" from the Boston & Albany.[14]

Ironically, James M. Stone had spoken with a principal of the Ware River about a possible combination. Charles Stevens, a Ware industrialist, and a director of the Ware River RR, testified that the problem with a combination in the Central's point of view was the route.   Stevens related that "Mr. Stone's objection was, that if they [the Central] did that [connect with the Ware River "a few miles from Palmer"], they could not call it the Massachusetts Central Road; they were going too near the Boston & Albany, and for that reason they diverged in another course, and got a longer and worse route [in West Hardwick], with higher grades."[15]

A New York group, headed by Chauncy Vibbard, held a large amount of Ware River stock and bonds by early 1872. Since the Boston & Albany RR, by charter, could not own the Ware River itself, Vice-President Lincoln later admitted that "it was suggested that if the president could secure a controlling interest in it, the directors would favor a lease of the road upon fair terms."[16]

Chester Chapin, along with some of his relatives and associates, proceeded to buy out the New Yorkers, and replaced them on the board of directors of the Ware River. They did not attempt to formally take over the Ware River in 1872, because, as Twichell later stated, the legislature would have withheld approval due to the influence of the Central.[17]

Since the Ware River was not making enough money to pay for its bonded debt, Chapin and his friends could legitimately foreclose on the property. They had the line put up for sale in the spring of 1873. Legislative authorization to create a new

Chester W. Chapin

corporation after the sale was obtained. The lease with the New London & Northern RR was voided because that line had violated it by not consulting with the Ware River directors at the time the former was leased to the Vermont Central RR.   As of April 1. 1873, the Boston & Albany operated the Ware River under a temporary agreement.

Chester Chapin bought the Ware River RR for $375,000 on May 28. A new corporation was formed, and new stock was exchanged for the old bonds.   Chapin used his own (and borrowed) funds, to complete the Ware River RR to its northern terminus at Winchendon. Negotiations for a lease to the Boston & Albany RR took place, officially between committees representing the two roads. Since Chapin was a principal in both lines, he was in the awkward position of seeming to be negotiating with himself!

According to Ginery Twichell, Chapin held off finalizing the lease until the Central "had ceased work" on its line in the autumn of 1873. Twichell felt that "the managers of the Massachusetts Central wielded a very great influence, and that they were decidedly opposed to the Boston & Albany Road, and decidedly opposed to all of the others."[18] Presumably, Twichell was referring to the Central's support in the legislature, due to the number of towns on its route. This block of legislators could have caused problems for the lease, as the Boston & Albany was partly owned by the state.

The lease was arranged late in 1873, by having the Boston & Albany RR pay a rental fee of a five (later seven) percent dividend on the valuation of the Ware River RR. While the lease was ratified by both railroads, Chapin's role in it was the subject of a legislative investigation in 1876. From the date of the lease, the Ware River RR was operated as a branch line of the Boston & Albany RR, and thus in hands unfriendly to the Central.

The Central's first priority in 1874 was to get an act through the legislature extending the time needed to complete it, and to allow it to hold its annual meetings in Boston. When the legislation was filed, the Central proudly pointed out that it was not seeking any monetary aid from the state.[19] The bill to allow meetings to be held in Boston was passed, although the time extension was not acted upon in that session.

A more trying political problem for the Central was the Hoosac Tunnel consolidation bill being considered by the legislature. Edward Dickinson of Amherst, a longtime supporter of the Central, "consented" to be nominated for a seat in the legislature for this session, even though he would be seventy one years old when it started.[20] His specific reason for doing so was to "look after the interests" of the Central, "in which he felt a deep concern."[21] Dickinson was named to the Joint Special Commitee considering the consolidation question.

The special committee reported out a bill in February that would allow for a consolidated railroad bewteen Troy and Boston. However, the state would retain ownership of the tunnel section, under trustees, who could liquidate the state's interest over ten years. Other lines wishing to connect with the tunnel (including the Central), would be allowed to do so. The bill was seen as a "good groundwork" to "satisfy all interests" in the matter.[22]

Stone gave an interview to a Springfield news reporter in early March to discuss the Central's position on the consolidation bill. The reporter had been told by "one of the officers of the road" that if the bill passed, "the Central will die, never to be resurrected," and that the money spent to build the road "had better been burned."[23] Stone told the reporter that it "made no particular difference" to the "speedy completion" of the Central if the consolidation bill passed. He declared "the falsity" of a rumor that the Fitchburg RR would "swallow up the Central." Stone expressed optimism that the Central would be completed soon, citing a proposed connection with the Springfiled, Athol. & NE RR that would garner traffic from Springfield for it. The straighter course and less hilly grades of the Central, plus its connection with lines on the north side of Boston were cited by Stone as justifying his faith in the Central's ability to compete with the Boston & Albany RR at Springfield.

The reporter quoted Stone's reaction to the story about the bill's effect on the line as "nonsense... about the road not being able to pay, or to talk of its dying without drawing its breath through the tunnel." If the tunnel was kept open to all, Stone would "guarantee" that the proposed connection to the tunnel line from Amherst "shall be done immediately." If the tunnel were to belong to the Fitchburg RR interests, it would make "no difference" if a Central extension ran from Amherst or Northampton toward the tunnel, as most of the traffic to the tunnel's west end would be under the control of the New York Central RR.   Stone felt that only an independent line on both sides of the tunnel would guarantee competitive freight rates on western goods. This was why the Boston & Albany RR did not oppose consolidation, as it obtained most of its traffic from the New York Central. For these reasons, "friends of the Central" in the legislature would oppose the consolidation.

Stone concluded the interview by stating that "the bonds of the Central are now being negotiated, and that such negotiations will soon be completed, either at home or abroad... to secure the immediate construction of the road."[24] Stone may have had some reason to believe this at the time, but the inability to market the line's bonds was to be the major stumbling block to resuming construction on the Central.

In May, 1874, a great flood on the Mill River damaged much property in North-ampton. This caused more grumbles about the cost of the town's debt incurred for the Central subscription. One report had the Central "dead beyond the hope of present resuscitation," leaving it unable to pay off bridge contractor John R. Smith. A "Central director" responded that the railroad had "met their ob-ligations in every case promptly," and that "the road will be finished."[25]

Friends of the Central mourned the passing of Edward Dickinson on June 16. On the day of his death, Dickinson was at his seat in the legislature, particpa-ting in debate on a bill to appropriate $3,000,000 to finish the Troy & Green-field railorad to the tunnel. His final speech had been to seek "a proper re-gard for the interest" of the Central. After he finished it, he fell ill, and returned to his boarding house, where he died that evening.[26] His daughter Emily, who outlived him by only a dozen years, would not become famous as a poet until decades later.

The legislature dealt with the consolidation issue by passing a bill to in-corporate the Boston, Hoosac Tunnel, & Western RR, which covered one of the western approaches to the tunnel. However, it did not "consolidate" any lines on the eastern side of the tunnel, nor did it let go of the state's interest in the tunnel.

Barre held a celebration to honor its centennial as a town on June 17, 1874. Rev. James Thompson, who delivered the historical address, used the occasion to make a jab at the Central. He pointed out that "two years ago, I was promised a delightful trip, three times a day, if I chose, over 'The Central Massachu-setts' to Barre Common, this very summer! I did not come by that route. I missed the train!"[27]

In July, The Central's appeal of the two year old judgement against it for damages to Hiram Tucker's Hardwick farm was heard. This was held under Special Coronor F.T. Blackmer, Esq. Tucker's counsel objected to jurors from Barre, as that town had subscribed for Central stock, so people from West Brookfield had to be substituted.[28] The jury awarded Blackmer $1,450 damages. The Central appealed this judgement.

That summer Henry Hills, a Central director from Amherst, was quoted as saying that if Norman Munson couldn't "fulfill his obligations speedily," that "Boston capital" would be supplied to finish the road. Hills also hinted the line would see "a probable new president before long."[29] This was the first public expression of dissatisfaction with Stone, which would gain momentum in later years. Munson was then working on a contract to grade and lay track in the Hoosac Tunnel, but no "capitalists" came forward to take up his stock in the Central.

Hills' statements may have reflected sentiment then current in Amherst to get the portion of the Central built between their town and Northampton. In feeling that "the prospects for the eastern division are just now somewhat dubious," it seemed that the town's $100,000 investment in the line would be returned by the "benefit" of this segment.[30] Unfortunately, the cost of finishing the Connecticut River bridge was too much for the Central to attempt at that time.

In October, a report circulated that Munson was notifying his subcontractors to be ready to return to work on the Central. It was presumed that he had obtained Boston money to back him up, but Central officials maintained "an ominous silence" regarding this false report, as well as on "the condition and prospects of the road."[31]

The Central's 1874 annual meeting, held in Boston on November 4, must have been a subdued affair. The directors' report showed that there was only $1,392 in cash in the company's coffers as of September 30. Only about $27,000 had been paid in on the stock during the previous year, while $276,000 of new unbonded liabilities had been incurred. The only steady source of income was a few thousand dollars in rents from company-owned housing.

It was reported that Barre, Hardwick, and Boylston had not paid the remainder of their assessments, but those tens of thousands of dollars would have been a mere drop in the bucket compared with what was needed to finish the Central. Stone expressed his by now cliched feeling that he "was confident that with the advent of better times, the bonds will be sold and the road built."[32] H.K. Starkweather, of Northampton, was elected to fill a seat on the board of directors.

A month after the annual meeting, there was a Central surveyor in Amherst, trying to find a new route that would accomodate the south village of that town. The local newspaper, after noting that the current location was the "most feasible route," satirized the ambitions of the south village by stating that the Central directors "will surely adopt that plan, and build an elegant depot on the green for the accomodation of newspaper correspondents."[33]

As 1874 came to an end, the Worcester & Nashua RR was reported to be trying to secure control of the Central. The Worcester & Nashua had just completed an extension to Rochester, NH, on the Maine border, which gave it dreams of becoming a major system. Since it crossed the Central's route in West Boylston, the Worcester & Nashua could complete the Central in order to gain a connection to the Hoosac Tunnel. However, the debt it incurred building the extension left the Worcester & Nashua in a weakened condition, so it was not able to persue the Central even if it wanted to.[34]

At the beginning of 1875, Norman Munson was dealt a financial blow that would send him on the road to bankruptcy. A decision was rendered in a court case on January 12 that concerned an event that took place on September 15, 1871. On that day, a scow belonging to Munson sank in Boston Harbor. The scow was hauling gravel for Munson to use in filling nearby mud flats, under a contract with the trustees of the Boston Hartford, and Erie RR. The filled area was to form part of that line's terminal facilities in Boston.

Two days after the scow sank, while it still sat in shallow water, the hulk was struck by the steamer *John Rohmer*, which suffered major damage. Munson had the scow refloated, but refused to compensate the Boston & Hingham Steamboat Company for the damage to its vessel. The steamboat company sued Munson, with the case reaching the state Supreme Court in November, 1874. Despite having Oliver Wendell Holmes, Jr. (later a judge on both the Massachusetts and U.S. Supreme Courts) on his legal team, Munson lost the case. This put a further large liability on his already overburdened financial resources.[35]

At the time this case was decided, Munson was awaiting final action in a suit he had filed against the bankrupt Boston, Hartford, & Erie RR. That line owed him $873,812,23 for contracting work. Recovering that sum would have gone far toward meeting his reported liabilities of over a million dollars. One small portion of his listed debts was $1,444 for wages, possibly from unpaid Central laborers.[36] With Munson in such financial straits, and holding a large amount of Central securities, work on the line would be held up at least until he could collect on his suit.

Problems with the Central's route in Amherst arose again in 1875. The South Amherst residents who had earlier expressed a desire that the Central pass through their village had a new survey done. This was shown to State Representative Isaac Stone, of Northampton, who filed a bill to authorize this change. The South Amherst parties argued that this new route would make a connecting line from Amherst to Deerfield easier to build. They cited a statement by Senator William Gaylord of Northampton that "The only way for the Central to ever amount to anything is the build the link from Amherst to the tunnel line." Of course, this did not sit well with Amherst Center citizens, and both sides sought a decision from the Central board of diretors, and watched the legislature to see what would happen to Stone's bill there.[37]

West of Amherst, a problem arose with the partially built bridge over the Connecticut River. James M. Stone, along with director Franklin Bonney of Hadley, attended a meeting with the Hampshire County Commissioners, and Selectmen from three area towns on February 15. All parties were concerned about erosion on the east bank of the river, near the bridge abutment.

It was agreed that the solution to the problem was to get the state to spend up to $30,000 to stabilize the river bank. A bill was filed to accomplish this, but the legislative committee reviewing it thought that the county should handle the matter. Stone thought the bill gave too much power to the county commissioners to assess shares of the cost onto interested parties (including the Central), so he opposed it.[38] Depsite Stone's objections, it passed with that proviso, which would mean another bill for the Central.

These concerns on the western end of the Central's route soon paled in the eyes of the Central directors when they got wind of the latest tunnel consolidation proposals. One was put forth by a group of Boston area businessmen, led by Edward Crane. They carried forth an 1873 consolidation proposal, known as the Boston & Northwestern RR, by forming a group known as the Bay State Transportation League. In a bill filed with the legislature in late 1874, they advocated the creation of a Boston & Chicago Railway Trust. This would combine the Fitchburg, Boston & Lowell, Mass, Central, Vermont & Mass., and Troy & Greenfield RRs with other roads and steamboat lines. The trust would be under state ownership, and create a new route between Boston & Chicago. In spite of an estimated cost of $54,000,000, it was given serious consideration by the legislature.

Another consolidation plan was put forth by the Boston, Hoosac Tunnel, & Western RR, one of the two lines which ran west from the tunnel to New York state. This proposal also included the Central as one of the two roads it would connect with east of the tunnel. In January, 1875, there was a report that "somebody is buying up the stock" of the Central "at a very low price." Many Central stockholders were said to be "glad to sell it for anything they can get, in the present discouraging condition of its affairs." The purchasers were reputedly acting "in the interest of the Boston, Hoosac Tunnel, Albany & Western Co., which proposes to build a new line from Boston to the Pennsylvania coal fields." If this were true, then the Boston & Hoosac Tunnel group may have been backing their play.[39]

There were two main reasons for these consolidation plans. One was to get better freight rates. The Boston & Albany RR was seen as not bringing in freight from the west as cheaply as it could be brought in through New York or Baltimore. This was due to its lack of competition for Boston business, which a consolidated line through the tunnel could supply. Another reason was to get the state out of being responsible for the tunnel and its maintenance, and to get a return on some of the huge sums it had invested there.[40]

James M. Stone testified at a legislative committee hearing on the Hoosac Tunnel in early February. He stated that neither he, nor any of his directors had been approached by the Hoosac Tunnel & Western RR about including the Central in their scheme. He stated that the Central directors "did not approve of the bill," nor did they "think that it is a proper solution of the Hoosac Tunnel problem."[41]

Stone asserted that the Central was still a viable proposition on its own, and that it did not wish to unite with any other line to or through the tunnel. Under the proposed bill, he felt that the Central could only "act as a club in the hands of the state, to allow the latter to drive a sharp bargain with the Fitchburg road." Stone saw no reason, under the bill, for the Central to build its own connection to the tunnel, for freight arrangements would be made "solely with the corporation controlling the tunnel."

In concluding his testimony, Stone mentioned possible connections with railroads west of the tunnel to the Pennsylvania coal fields. This comment may have aroused suspicions about the Central stock purchase rumor. But when he was asked about the Central connecting to the tunnel from Amherst or Northampton, Stone would only admit that Munson had "on his own account" investigated a connection with the tunnel.[42]

After several more hearings, a "toll gate" bill for the Hoosac Tunnel passed the legislature in late March. This would have allowed any railroad reaching either end of the tunnel line to use it by paying the state a toll. This did not satisfy any of the parties interested in the matter, which meant that the subject would come before the legislature again.

Stone made another appearance before the legislature in March, seeking a two year extension of the deadline for completion of the Central. Amherst parties were split over a provision allowing the Central to change its route there. This change would put the route close to both Amherst and South Amherst villages. This had been filed by Rep. Isaac Stone of Northampton, at the behest of "300 or so citizens" of Amherst, many from the south village. The representative from Belchertown also favored the change, as he felt that it would assist the promotion of the proposed line from his town to Holyoke. Some felt that the change would assist the building of a branch from Amherst toward the tunnel line.[43]

Stone stated that the "majority of the directors would favor the change, as it would help the road as well as the town." However, he added, "having filed their location there, and having had considerable difficulty in securing Amherst's subscription," the directors wouldn't change the route. Stone also indicated that the Central "would now be finished within a year."[44] The time extension bill (form two years) passed with the authorization to change the Amherst route, leaving that town to wonder where the Central route would be located there.

Some of Stone's doubletalk on the Amherst to Deerfield extension did not escape notice. In May, a reporter for a Northampton newspaper ridiculed Stone's statements during the previous winter that the Central would be "done within eight months." The reporter noted the "nothing has been done... nor is there any prospect of anything being done at once." He felt that the only reason for delay was "to allow for further prefecting of plans and combinations by which the Central is to be benefitted." He thought it "absurd" that Stone stated that "the Central does not desire to make any arrangement with the state for a great through line."

The reporter thought that Stone's opposition to the Central being part of any through route was because it would make "'Othello's occupation gone,' and the $4,000 salary gone with it." He quoted "friends of the Central" in their "dissatisfaction with the dilly-dallying of its officers." He urged the towns along the route, as major stockholders in the line, to "criticize the do-nothing policy of the Central, and demand that something be done."[45]

A letter-writer to the *Barre Gazette* three months later expressed the same mood. He advised that the directors of the Central should "get a different man at the head of the board for President, one that has the vim in him to go on, and complete the road, and my impression is that people will be much better pleased than by any other arrangement." To be fair to Stone, the fact that Norman Munson's finances were still a mess prevented construction from resuming, as did the inability to market the Central's bonds. Perhaps the latter activity could have been pursued more agressively.[46]

Whether or not Stone was aware of these criticisms of him, he did take some action to improve the Central's position. As early as January of thet year, a Boston newspaper had hinted about the benefits of a new direct route from Boston to the coal fields of Pennsylvanis. This would cross the Hudson River via a bridge to be built at Poughkeepsie, New York. Boston surveyor H.T. Keith was sent out during the summer and early autumn to find a route between Westfield and the extreme southwestern corner of the state. Central directors also consulted with directors of the paper Lee & New Haven and Lee & Hudson railroads about possible connections with parts of their lines. Ironically, these three railroads were the only ones in the state to have "entirely stopped construction" at this time![47] The ultimate goal of this scheme was to connect with the Poughkeepsie & Eastern RR, which reached the eastern terminus of the proposed bridge.

While the Central was flirting with wild schemes to expand itself, Edward Crane of the Bay State Transportation League went across the state to promote his massive consolidation scheme. He must have viewed towns along the Central's route as likely recruiting grounds for supporters, for Crane spoke in several of them. A "fair audience" heard him in Barre at the beginning of August. He spoke of "cheap transportation" as the only way to keep industries from "lying idle" and "secure prosperity to the state." Pushing his plan for state-owned railways, he sought "the people first, the corporations afterwards." He concluded the meeting by passing out pamphlets outlining the proposed railway trust.[48]

The   *Springfield Republican* observed that Crane's "tour" was "too late" to have   any   effect.   It sarcastically noted that the "Central people are disposed to   clutch   at it as the saving straw, but it is only a straw, and nobody has got hold   of   the other end."   In their view, "The State won't hear of it... finally Boston   has   wearied   of Crane, and ceased to believe that pots of gold underlie the butresses of his rainbows."[49]

Crane spoke in Amherst on October 28, pointing out that the town was taxed $2,220   a   year to support the Hoosac Tunnel, without receiving any benefit from it. The townspeople may have been more interested in the race for the State Senate.   One   candidate,   Rep.   Isaac Stone, of Northampton, was called to account for   supporting   the   desires   of   South   Amherst to change the Central route in their   favor.   This Stone may have made some enemies in Amherst, as he lost the election a week later.[50]

The   Central suffered another minor setback that autumn, as the Hiram Tucker   land   case   wound   up its final court appearance.   The Central had filed exceptions   to the evidence in the jury trial on the case.   Specifically, the Central   objected   to   testimony   by one of Tucker's farmer neighbors about the effect of the railroad on Tucker's land.

Judge   Brigham of the Superior Court had ruled in late 1874 to allow the exceptions,   but   failed   to decide the case.   The state Supreme Court had to rule that   the   exceptions were not in its jurisdiction. This brought the case back to the   Superior   Court, where Judge Colburn gave Tucker his award.   The Central appealed   this   to the Supreme Court, but they allowed the farmer's testimony, and confirmed   Tucker's   award.   Not only did this cost the Central several hundred dollars   for the higher award, but the legal fees must have eaten up more of the railroad's precious funds!

The   annual meeting of the Central took place in Boston at the beginning of November.   The stagnation of the line was reflected in the same officers and directors   being re-elected.   The finance committee, consisting of directors Brigham   and   Cutting,   and   contractor   Munson,   reported "little encouragement" in their attempts to market the Central's bonds.[51]

The railroad's annual report to the state showed that 446 of the line's 451 stockholders   were   from Massachusetts.   The financial statement showed that the Central   had   taken   in $2,645.96 in rents during the previous twelve months, but had   spent over $10,000 on surveys. It also showed the Central had $69,250 worth of bond coupons "overdue and unpaid."

As   1875   came to a close, the final surveys for extending the Central from Westfield   to the New York border were displayed.   The 53 mile route would make Great   Barrington   closer to Boston than Pittsfield was, at an estimated cost of about $4,000,000.   As one newspaper cynically reported, "Berkshire is in the exhibit,   nevertheless   -   where's   the   money coming from?"[52]   Stone mentioned a possible   "branch   line" to Holyoke (with the potential connection to the Poughkeepsie   Bridge   route)   in   a statement written in early 1876,   confirming that this was a serious option for the Central.[53]

The   national centennial year of 1876 began with the Central the subject of fresh rumors.   Several   newspapers   ran a story indicating that "somebody" was buying   up Central stock at ten cents on the dollar.   There was much speculation over   who   was   trying to "capture" the Central, including one or two groups who wanted   to   tie   it   in   with the tunnel line.   Another suggested speculator was Chester Chapin, of the Boston & Albany RR, who would tie the line in with a project he was rumored to be considering to connect with Providence, R.I.[54]

A statement scotching these rumors appeared in the *Boston Herald* at the end of January. Possibly issued by the Central (or Stone), it asserted that, since most of the stock in the line was held by towns, there was little likelihood that anyone could buy a controlling interest in it. The Central was compared with many other businesses in that "generally stagnant" economy, "waiting for the moving of the waters." The surveys to connect the Central with either the tunnel line or the Poughkeepsie bridge route were cited as proof of its "importance" for its "ease in working and shortness of route" to the west.[55]

Unfortunately for the Central, such explanations were no longer accepted at face value by many of those interested in the line. Members of the legislature were agitated into investigating the affairs of several railroads in the state, including the Eastern, Boston & Albany, and the Central. One reporter thought that the Central "will be hauled over the coals, and President Stone asked to explain where the money subscribed by numerous towns has gone to."[56] Another stated that "the opinion prevails among many that President Stone and Contractor Munson made a good thing out of the operation, making little financial difference to them whether the road was built or not."[57] As it turned out, the Central itself would not be investigated, but it would be brought up in connection with the Boston & Albany probe, and an investigation of a railroad commissioner.

The investigation of the Boston & Albany RR was conducted because of the perceived confilct of interest of Chester Chapin in the lease of the Ware River RR. The Boston & Albany had state directors, who had not (with one exception) found anything wrong with Chapin's dual role; one even helped Chapin's project with funds! During the course of the hearings on this, several of the witnesses cited the threat of competition from the Central as the main reason for the B&A to aquire the Ware River RR.*

The other investigation ended up putting the Central in a bad light. This was held to examine Railroad Commissioner A. D. Briggs' conflict in taking contracts for bridge construction from railroads in the state. The sorest point to some was Briggs' firm being involved with the Central bridge over the Connecticut River. During the hearings on this, James M. Stone testified that he knew "nothing" of the specifics of the bridge contract. This was not believed by all, and if it was true, it made Stone look like a bad manager.[58]

Later testimony in the Briggs investigation revealed Munson's $6,000 payoff to the Northampton trio to give the Connecticut River bridge contract to Briggs' partner. This reflected poorly on Munson and the three Northampton men. Luke Lyman, the most eminent of the trio, was ridiculed by a few newspapers near Northampton, although not by his hometown one. The sharpest jab was made in a rare editorial cartoon in the *Amherst Record*, which depicted Lyman as a carpetbagger.[59]

While there were calls for Lyman to resign his post as Register of Probate, or to have him investigated, none of this came to pass. Lyman remained a respected local citizen for the rest of his life. The fact that the Central was inactive, and that the money invested by Northampton, Hadley, and Amherst could have been used to build a local line connecting those towns was again brought up by the Central's enemies in that region. This would come to haunt James M. Stone, as he would no longer enjoy the support of directors from these towns.

The investigation ended up exhonorating Commissioner Briggs of any wrongdo-

----

* See pp. 41-3.

Editorial Cartoon in the Amherst Bulletin, April 5, 1876

ing. However, it recommended legislation to prevent a railroad commissioner from doing any business with a railroad in the state. In another action, the legislature voted to extend the time limit for those filing claims aganist the Central for another year.

Norman Munson's luck finally ran out around the time he testified during the Briggs investigation. He filed for bankruptcy, having previously assigned his contracts on the Hoosac Tunnel line to two of his bondholders, Franklin Haven and Benjamin Bates. Munson's career would not be over, but he would no longer be the major contractor he once was.

The Central won a case against another railroad decided by the state Supreme Court in October. This involved the erection of piers for a bridge in Berlin to allow the Central to pass over the Boston, Clinton & Fitchburg RR line. The latter railroad won a small sum for property damage, but sought to have the Central pay for the stationing of a flagman at a nearby road crossing. This was required by the county commissioners when the town contended that the piers obstructed the view of people at the crossing. The court found that the flagman might not always be needed, so it threw out the requirement that the Central pay for it.

In spite of a third straight year of inactivity on the Central, citizens of South Amherst still pushed to get the route shifted in their favor. A "very fully attended meeting" on this subject was held there on November 6, 1876. It resolved that local legislators "use their influence" to secure the route change. Having noted the qualms of the town center regarding their ambitions, the resolve also asked that the route "to the middle of the town [be] as direct as may be." The secretary of the meeting indicated to the local newspaper that his section wanted to "share" the Central with the center, not keep it from there. Unfortunately, this effort was moot until the Central resumed construction.[60]

The annual meeting of the Central was held on December 6, in Boston. The report to the Railroad Commissioners, made on September 30, showed an income for

the year, from rents, of $1,615.43.   Expenses incurred included $6,413.83 for
"engineering, agencies, salaries, and other," which must have included the surveys made in the Berkshires.

Norman Munson reported that he had "just got through insolvency," and that
he was "anxious to go on with his contract" with the Central.   Munson did not
know if he could take up the work in "thirty days... or that it might be six
months," but he "had no reasonable doubt" that he could do it. He further emphasized that this had been the only contract in his career that he had "failed to
fulfill."[61]

When it came time to elect the directors, General Otis, of Northampton was
chosen to succeed L.J. Starkweather, who had moved out of that town.   The votes
of Northampton and Hadley were cast against James M. Stone for re-election as a
director, but he prevailed.   Stone and the other officers were re-elected to
their positions.   Some people present at the meeting "threw out insinuations"
about the honesty of the directors.   Enos Parsons of Northampton offered a motion to form a committee to investigate such charges, but it was not se-
conded.   Parsons then stated that he hoped "no more insinuations of that kind
would be made without foundation."[62]   When Parsons' action was misinterpreted
by some, he wrote a letter to a newspaper. stating he had offered the motion to
give the "insinuators" the "fullest opportunity to satisafy themselves."   Parsons indicated that he shared the public's "disappointment" in the lack of progress on the Central.   However, he reiterated his faith in the officers of the
company, and expressed the hope that Munson could "realize his expectations" to
complete the line soon.[63]

The tide began to turn strongly against Stone in January. 1877, with the pub-
lication of several newspaper articles questioning his motives as the President
of the Central.   It was reported that at a meeting of the line's board of directors held early that month, questions raised about the finances of the line
by the directors from Northampton, Hadley, and Amherst were "snubbed" by
Stone.   If anyone tried to find out about "points of financial interest," they
were "at once charged with being an enemy of the road."   Upon further inquiry,
these directors were shown the Central's account books, "from which, of course,
only an expert could extract the truth."[64]

The directors from the western towns thought that they could vote in some new
directors, and a new president, but learned that the Central's by-laws allowed
Stone to use Norman Munson's partially paid-up stock, acting as proxy, to
outvote any action he deemed inimical to his interests.   Munson had obtained
most of his stock for work performed, and it was charged that he was overpaid
$200,000 in stock and bonds before the assigned work was finished.   Stone's
$4,000 annual salary waa seen as a drain on the Central, as money had to be
borrowed to pay for it.

There was talk of the aggrieved directors seeking an injunction from the
state Supreme Court to prevent Stone from further involvement in running the
line, and of an investigation of its affairs by the legislature's railroad committee.   However, neither of these actions took place, as it waa decided to
give him another year "to redeem his numerous promises, especially as he is the
'ring,' diameter, and circumference" of the Central.[65]

The only action the legislature took in regard to the Central in 1877 was to
consider the road's petition for another two year extension of its deadline.
Stone testified at the railroad committee hearing on this in late February.   He
stressed the ability of the corporation to finish the line within the two year
extension sought, "although he failed to state the grounds of his confidence."

This observer further reported that "the sole reliance of the company is on its bonds, the negotiation of which just now would be a difficult matter."[66]

While the Central's petition was under consideration, Edward Crane's railway trust proposal (including an extended Central as an element) was competing with a tunnel consolidation plan presented by General William Burt of the Boston, Hoosac Tunnel & Western RR. Burt's line, on its New York end, was inching toward a connection with the West Shore RR, which would open a route to the west. He offered to lease the railroads east of the tunnel, but leave it open for other lines to use, on a toll basis. Burt also offered his solution to the tunnel problem as the only one not dependent upon the New York Central RR for business.[67] While neither scheme was approved, the Central did get its construction deadline extended to May 1, 1879.

A new stroke of bad luck hit the Central when a heavy windstorm hit Northampton on June 14, 1877. Besides causing a great deal of damage in that area, the "tornado" blew the unfinished framework off of the piers on the Central's bridge over the Connecticut River. The adjacent highway bridge was also destroyed by the storm. The debt burden that would be imposed to rebuild the latter bridge caused a local newspaper to comment that this was the latest in "a series of calamities" that commenced with Northampton's vote to subscribe to the Central in 1870.[68] Unfortunately, the ruined Central bridge would stand for another decade as a reminder of the unfinished railroad.

That spring, negotiations to sell the Central's remaining bonds were taking place under "the utmost secrecy," during which "all sorts of rumors derogatory to the management had to be submitted to in silence."[69] It appears that one Matthews, a Boston real estate investor, "got heavily loaded" with Central bonds (from Munson?), and was trying to use them to pay off his creditors. Matthews was not offered much for them, possibly because anyone trying to buy them to gain control of the Central had to deal with the "menace" of Stone's holding $1,700,000 of unissued bonds.[70]

The Central's directors came up with a scheme to call in all of the bonds, and issue new ones at a lower rate of interest. This may have been done to obtain a higher par value on the bonds, and to relieve Matthews of his huge portion. A new contract was also made with Munson to finish the line within twelve months of commencing work.

In spite of this burst of apparent activity, no new work on the Central commenced in 1877. A glowing puff piece, based upon notes compiled by Stone, appeared in the *Boston Traveller* in late June. Titled "Independent Line to the West," it sought local investors in the Central by demonstrating the advantages of "the control and management of the active businessmen of Boston" in what would be a "profitable investment."[71]

Perhaps no "active businessmen of Boston" took Stone up on the offer, as it was reported a few weeks later that General Burt, of the Hoosac Tunnel & Western RR, had purchased $900,000 of the Central's bonds. He was said to have paid Munson and Matthews less than $120,000 for them.[72] If true, this would have made sense for Burt, as he was frustrated in his attempts to gain control of lines east of the tunnel. The Central, with the extension to Shelburne Falls, would have given him a line to Boston.

Whether or not Burt was the purchaser of the Central bonds, a wave of change swept over the Central at its annual meeting on November 1. Five new directors from New York, and one from Boston were added to the board, joining most of the former ones. The New Yorkers were Andrew H. Green, a comptroller for the City of New York; Darius Mangam and Joseph Pool, both bank presidents; Daniel Sprague, a broker; and Josiah Reed, a businessman who was a native of Northampton. The Bostonian, John Woolredge, had made a fortune in shoe manufacturing, and was once President of the Eastern RR.

The election of the new directors may have been arranged by Norman Munson as a way of obtaining New York financing for the Central. It was reported that Stone had arranged for these new members, and that Green would replace him as President. Stone was supposed to have sought to "volunarily retire from that position," for "several years" but that the then "directors would not consent to it."[73] This seems unlikely, in light of subsequent events. Munson may have simply refused to let Stone vote his stock for the latter's benefit.

One newspaper felt that the results of the annual meeting indicated "some subtantial power is now at the helm," and that "the new management means business" in completing the line and connecting it with both the Hoosac Tunnel and the Poughkeepsie Bridge route. An ominous note for Stone was the adjournment of the meeting for a month "to give the new directors time to look into the affairs of the road."[74]

Rumors about possible combinations of the Central with other lines flew as 1877 came to a close. The planned directors' meeting was postponed, reportedly because the New York Central RR was interested in finishing the Mass. Central to head off William Burt's scheme of a Boston to Chicago railway through the Hoosac Tunnel.[75] One newspaper reported that Amherst townspeople "care little now who finishes the Central... give us the road and we will be only too well content."[76] The meeting may have been postponed due to the fact that the newly elected directors had turned down the positions.

1878 would see many changes in the Mass. Central, including the end of Stone's career with it. One of the Central's first actions that year was to seek payment of unpaid assessments. Barre was told to pay up, or its stock would be sold off.[77] A town meeting was held in Barre in late January, which resolved not to pay the assessments. A commitee of three, iuncluding Central stockholder Austin Adams, was appointed to protect the town's interest in the matter. They secured a postponement of the stock sale, but another town meeting still refused payment. The committee (with a replacement for Adams) was authorized to sue the railroad if it attempted to sell the stock.

Besides seeking funds from unpaid assesments, the board sought viable candidates to replace the unwilling New York directors. The adjourned directors meeting was finally held in late March. Three new directors from New York, and two from Northampton and Amherst were nominated with the votes of the stockholders from the western towns. Stone "accused the western men of treachery and underhanded work," but this did not prevent the calling of a stockholders meeting for April 3 to ratify these changes.[78]

Who were these new directors? One, Northampton's Luke Lyman, had just supervised the completion of the new highway bridge over the Connecticut River. W. A. Dickinson, of Amherst, was a relative of the late Edward Dickinson. The New Yorkers were Milton Courtwright, financier Thomas C. Durant, and Silas Seymour.

Seymour was a relative of former New York Governor and 1868 Presiential candidate Horatio Seymour. Born in Stillwater, NY in 1817, Seymour worked his way up from axeman to division engineer of the Erie RR. He served as an engineer for other New York lines until 1855, when he was elected State Engineer and Surveyor. Upon the outbreak of the Civil War, Seymour helped General Dan Sickles organize the Excelcior Brigade, and obtained a the rank of Colonel for himself.

During the war, Seymour did some engineering work in Washington D.C. He was appointed by Thomas Durant as a consulting engineer for the Union Pacific RR in 1865. Some considered him Durant's "spy." He was described as "dandified," with "an aristocratic air." Indians along the route of the Union Pacific were amused at the sight of Seymour in his silk hat, carrying a sun umbrella, ac-

Silas Seymour
(Simonhoff, *Sketches of Men of Mark*)

companied by a mistress and Black servants. As a consulting engineer, Seymour was not highly regarded by Chief Engineer Grenville Dodge. Seymour showed that he "knew very little about railroad construction" and "lacked the drive" to build the line fast enough in its early stages.[79] Seymour may have been distracted by the book he was writing about his observations along the Union Pacific, published in 1867.

Seymour's image belied his abilities as a crafty promoter, who proposed circuitous routes for the Union Pacific in order to obtain more government grant money. He got kickbacks from some of the railroad's contractors, and used a "booster style" to promote the project.[80] Seymour was present at the driving of the Golden Spike cere-mony uniting the Union Pacific and the Central Pacific RRs in 1869.* His ca-reer after that time was less glamorous, so he accepted the offer to join the Central's board of directors.

Before the meeting on April 3, 1878, stockholders from the Central's western towns held their own informal meeting, and "went down ready to push things." At the official meeting, held at the company's Boston office, they rebuffed the suggestion of "an eastern man" that the Central be put through to Hudson first. They were tired "of being told to wait and wait... they have waited in vain." [81] The line's by-laws were changed to provide for better stockholder representation on the board of directors. The new directors, including Seymour, were then confirmed, bringing the total to sixteen.

Immediately following the stockholders meeting, the directors met. Stone, presumably realizing that the game was up, resigned as President and as a director. Silas Seymour was then elected President, with "hopes that, being rid of President Stone, something may be done for the road." While there was little confidence that the money needed to complete the line could "be raised at once," Seymour and Munson set out at once to survey the route to determine the practicality of renewing construction.[82]

----

* Ironically, this was held on the same day (May 10) that the Mass. Central's charter was granted.

Chapter Five   REVIVAL

Soon after Stone's ouster, the Central received good news in the form of a legal settlement its favor. This was on a suit the Central brought against the town of Wayland for not paying the assessments on its stock subscription. This may have caused by manufacturers in Cochituate village, who had wanted a Central branch built for them. The federal district court ruled in favor of the railroad in the spring of 1877, awarding it $42,000. However, the town brought exceptions to the award to the U. S. Supreme Court, which had not yet heard the case.

It appears that James Draper, longtime Central director and clerk, urged his town to settle with the railroad for $32,500. The committee of the town handling the matter counteroffered $30,000. The attorney for the Central director who brought the suit (apparently Henry Hills), without consulting any other directors, offered to accept $40,000. James Stone later asserted that he personally urged the three directors handling the matter to accept no less than $40,000. The figure agreed upon, in the spring of 1878, was $37,500. The attorneys handling the case took out $5,350 for their fees.[1]

Silas Seymour wasted no time in attempting to revive the Central. He came up with a plan, which was first broached to the directors in early May. This was to put the stock of the line in the hands of a trustee to get the road completed. The stockholders would still retain their voting powers. If the trustee did not complete the line within two years of the transfer, it would revert back to the stockholders. If it was completed, one quarter of it would revert, and the other three-quarters would be conveyed as the directors saw fit.

This plan was approved at a stockholders meeting held In early June. Former Governor Thomas Talbot agreed to serve as the trustee. Talbot, of Billerica, was the son-in-law of former Central director Joel Hayden. Approval for the transfer was obtained from the municipalities holding stock by early summer. Julius Hartwell presided at the Northampton meeting where this was considered. Charles Delano and others offered amendments to the motion, trying to protect the town's interests, and to guarantee that the Central would be built to Northampton. When Delano attacked the line's management under Stone, L.J. Dudley and Enos Parsons defended the current course of the directors, and asked that the stock proposal be approved as submitted.[2] This was done at a meeting a week later, with some minor stipulations added to protect the town.

James Joslin, a Hudson attorney (and later a director) for the Central, canvassed the towns along the route to obtain the shares of individual stockholders. In Barre, he obtained 252 shares from 31 people. About 2,400 shares were obtained from other individuals. The appointed agents for eight of the towns, representing 6,339 shares, turned them over to the trustee in late July.

In an attempt to interest potential investors in the Central's securities, Silas Seymour issued a 30 page prospectus in July. A map appended to this document not only included the main route of the Central, but the projected extensions to Holyoke and the tunnel line. Connections with the existing Springfield & NE, Boston, Barre & Gardner, and Worcester & Nashua RRs were emphasized, as were proposed connections with a line from Worcester and Berlin, and one running north from North Brookfield.

Seymour's arguments in favor of the Central's ability to pay dividends were mostly the same ones used by James M. Stone over the years. Ironically, two-thirds of the pamphlet was taken up by statements written by Stone in 1876 and 1877! A table at the end of the pamphlet indicated that of fifteen major communities in Massachusetts and New York, the Central would provide the shortest route to Boston for ten of them, and be less than five miles longer than existing routes for four others.

As part of an effort to gather in any other possible assets, the new board of directors asked James M. Stone to return $37,000 worth of bonds he held in lieu of several years unpaid salary as President. Stone refused to return the bonds, contending that he was offered less in settlement for them than others received.[3] Stone attempted to auction off the bonds on October 5, but was restrained by a court order obtained by the directors. Judge Ames, of the State Supreme Court, declared that it had not been legal for the Central to issue bonds as collateral security for its notes.

The Central held its tenth annual meeting on October 30. J.W. Rollins, of Boston was elected to replace Thomas Durant on the board. The other fourteen board members were re-elected. The treasurer's report showed that in the previous year, notes and accounts payable were reduced by $37,541, and $2,244.80 was received from stock sales. However, expenses continued to mount in the form of additional engineering costs, contingent account, and interest payments. This did not include the unpaid coupons on the bonds. The cash on hand totalled $4,357.80.

A committee of five was appointed to revise the corporation's by-laws. The meeting was adjourned for a week to hear their report. The directors then met to re-elect Seymour as President. The proposed by-laws changed several practices of the Central which had come under criticism during Stone's tenure. A quorum of five directors was established, with each being required to be a stockholder, or represent a town's shares. Two of the directors, and the President, were to form a finance committee. The treasurer was required to make monthly reports to the directors, and not disburse any funds (including promissory notes) without their approval.

The annual meeting reconvened on November 6. James M. Stone was present, and offered an amendment to the proposed by-laws, forbidding directors from serving on committees on matters in which "their private interest is involved, distinct from the general interest of the corporation." Stone delivered a long speech to explain his reasons for the amendment. In it, he accused some of the directors of paying themselves over half of the money received from of the stock subscription settlement with Wayland earlier that year.[4]

Stone accused the three dirctors of having "clutched the money to pay to themselves two-thirds of all the company owed them" for Central bonds, but no one else's (including Stone's bonds). Stone referred to this incident to defend his attempt to sell his bonds by stating, "After such an exhibition of the doings of the directors of a practically insolvent corporation, in making preferred creditors of themselves, any creditor outside of the charmed circle of such a board of directors would be justified in securing his own interest in any lawful manner. The "bare quorum of stockholders" and five directors present voted to table Stone's amendment "for future action."[5] This would be James M. Stone's last known public involvement with the Central.

The new Central board of directors negotiated with the Boston & Lowell RR to provide them with terminal facilities in Boston. The Central wanted the other line to provide a guarantee fund for construction, but the Boston & Lowell was not interested in making this investment. Since Central trustee Thomas Talbot (just elected to another term as Governor) was "considerably interested" in the Boston & Lowell, it was easy to reach an agreement with that road to operate the Central "at least as far as Hudson," when it was built,[6]

As the year 1878 came to an end, it was reported that the Central would push for an extension from Amherst to the tunnel. The only solace left for North-ampton was the contemplated construction of the connection to the tunnel line by the New Haven and Northampton RR. A contract was let by Munson late in the year to John Dow to complete work on the portion of the line from Stony brook to Hudson. One of Dow's gangs of men began the first work on the line in five years around Christmastime.[7]

The beginning of work on the Central caused a "cheerful feeling to exist" in Waltham, This was seen to increase when the surveyors had the town "safely cut through" for the extension east to Cambridge.[8] Munson, after reportedly re-ceiving $400,000 in funds to work with, awarded a contract for grading work from Hudson to Oakdale to contractors Gardner & Flynn. The only real obstacle they faced was a "large piece of rock work" in Berlin.[9]

In January 1879, the Central petitioned the legislature to extend the dead-line for construction for another two years. It also sought to have its chart-er amended to allow it to build the contemplated extensions northwest from Am-herst to Deerfield, and east from Stony brook to Cambridge. When hearings were held on the petition, the Fitchburg RR lobbied hard against the two route additions. That line did not want any other railroad to connect with the tunnel route, and it didn't want the Central's competition west from Boston.[10]

In response to the Fitchburg RR's charges, the Central published a pamphlet to refute them. It pointed out that it needed the authorization to build the ex-tensions in order to get the funding to finish the main line. In answer to a charge that there had been "irregularities" in the stock subscriptions, the com-pany offered to let anyone inspect its books, as the charge was "without found-ation."[11]

The Fitchburg RR asserted that the Central did not need a line east of the connection with theirs at Stony Brook, as they would provide the needed access to Boston. In the pamphlet, Silas Seymour reproduced correspondence between him-self and President William Stearns of the Fitchburg when this possibility was explored in 1878. First, Stearns offered to connect his main line with the Cen-tral via. his Marlboro Branch in Hudson, citing reduced costs to the Central to do this. Of course, that would have eliminated the Central's traffic (and sub-scriptions) from towns east of Hudson. When Seymour pointed this out, Stearns replied that, "since the distance is so short that you would run over our road (east of Stony Brook), our board think that it will be of no use for our com-pany to offer any terms for such facilities, feeling satisfied that we cannot make any terms that will be satisfactory to your company."[12]

As Seymour stated it, the Central could have excercised its charter right to use the Fitchburg tracks east of Stony Brook, "but this would have involved a compulsory arrangement with an unfriendly and competing company, and the result would have been unprofitable and unpleasant to both parties."[13]

One last argument against the extension east of Stony Brook was the objection of some landowners along the route. Petitions from Belmont, Newton, and Wal-tham contained a total of 116 names opposing the line. The Waltham petition in-dicated a belief that the grade crossings on the Central's route there "would interfere with public travel." On the other hand a petition from Belmont fav-oring the Central had an equal number of names, while twelve petitions from Waltham favoring the line contained 796 names. It was also pointed out that the Central's route in those towns would not cross any other railroad at grade.[14]

The Central's arguments won out, as the legislation it sought was passed in late April. This extended the line's time limit until May 1, 1881, and authorized the two extensions. The western extension was not to be completed until the Central had finished its original route to Northampton. A new survey on the latter route was already completed. It showed a line of "easy grades" thirteen miles long, from Amherst to West Deerfield.[15]

That spring, the Central missed out on what could have been a useful investment. The Springfield, Athol, & NE RR was foreclosed upon by its bondholders. Chief among them were Willis Phelps, who had constructed much of the line, and Chester Chapin of the Boston & Albany RR. The line was put up for sale on May 22, 1879, and Phelps purchased it (reportedly for himself and Chapin) for $395,000.[16] This wiped out more than $750,000 in stock, much of which was held by the towns and individuals along the route.

Phelps & Co. reorganized this line as the Springfield & NE RR. Now that it was free of the old debts, they negotiated with the Boston & Albany to have it purchased for a branch line. This action would eliminate the fear of the Boston & Albany that the Central could make use of this line to gain Springfield traffic.[17]

This sequence of events was typical of the sharp practices of the "robber baron" era. As historian Gustavus Myers put it, if capitalists "desired a railroad to be on a paying basis, they, as stockholders, took its dividends; if it suited their ulterior purposes to bankrupt it, they, as bondholders, could foreclose, and buy it back at a bargain price. In the phrase of the street, they could 'play both ends against the middle.'"[18] The only reasons this didn't happen to the Central were Munson's holding such a large amount of stock, and the fact that it was unfinished. In any case, the Central's prostrate condition again prevented it from buying up a useful connection at a bargain price.

The Central made a new contract with Norman Munson in June. He was to pay the remainder of the money due for the assessments on his stock, buy $500,000 more from the Central, and be paid $3,500,000 upon completion of the road. The terms of this agreement would not be fully carried out, but it shows the faith the Central directors had in Munson's "high position... in the financial and commercial community." A pamphlet was issued by the directors to publicize this arrangement, in the hopes that it would encourage investment in the Central's securities.[19]

A potential cost-cutting move was undertaken with a new survey that summer. To bypass the long route through West Hardwick, Greenwich, and Enfield, an alternate one through Ware and Bondsville was examined. The new route would save at least two-and-a-half miles in distance, be easier to build, and "afford a great deal more business" to the Central than it could get in Greenwich and Enfield.[20]

There was "earnest discussion" about the route change in Ware, including the potential for a "large outlay for land damages." While some thought that the Central should tie in with, or parallel the Ware River RR there, one letter writer from Ware favored the original route. "Observer" thought that "to construct two roads so near together... when 'there is not half business enough for one road to do it bad economy.'"[21]

Another Ware letter writer thought that wealthy elements in the town would oppose the Central's coming there. If not, "it would be crowded out as far as possible, so as to prevent its being of much practical benefit." He thought it would be routed through the "dooryard of a mechanic or a farmer," but "not through the garden of one manufacturer, or the front yard of the agent of another."[22]

While the change of the route was being considered, further action was being taken to make the Central a reality. In August, orders were placed for locomotive tenders, freight and passenger cars with various companies. A stockholders meeting accepted the law for the extensions, and authorized a mortgage of $2,700,000. The directors formally voted to "make permmanent arrangements for its business to and from the west" via. the tunnel route.[23]

The change of the route to Ware may also have been "fully decided" at this meeting, as it was considered a "settled fact" by the end of September.[24] This raised the problem of Hardwick's stock subscription, which was only two-fifths paid up.   The subscription had been made on the premise that the route would follow the original course through West Hardwick. It was reported that the Central was willing to settle with the town by releasing it from paying the money, if the town would surrender the stock. The town would not agree to do this. Opinion in Enfield was mixed: some feared the line would skip them, while others were "grumbling becuase they fear it will go here."[25]

One rumor held that, since the Central was breaking the conditions of the subscription by changing the route, that Hardwick could get its money back. As one newspaper asked "Where,oh where are they going to get it back? by suing the railroad company and attaching what Barre is to pay, or the roadbed in the west part of town?" It was asserted that the county commissioners had prepared two separate sets of land damage awards in West Hardwick, depending upon whether the route of the Central was changed or not.[26]

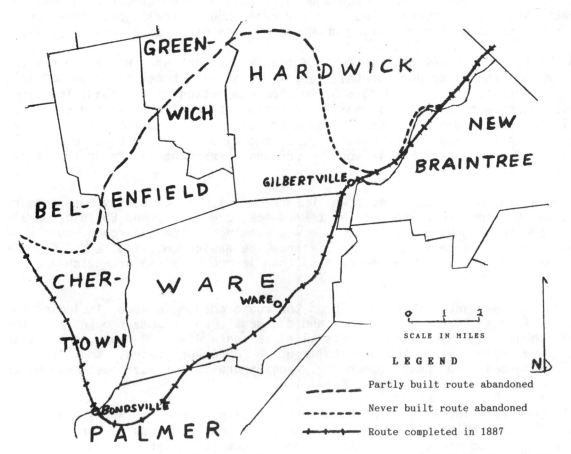

Map of the Central Route Change in the Ware and Swift River Valleys

A Hardwick reporter wrote a rueful comment about the changing of the Central route to the south.   He felt that this change would "doom West Hardwick to obscurity and [leave] the unsightly marks of misdirected industry and capital to be of no earthly use except, perhaps, to puzzle the future antiquarian." The writer further mused, "Imagine that collector of musty manuscripts, and dealer in mummies and old bones, scratching his head over the problem 2000 years hence, and after deciphering the hieroglyphics and studying the fossils of the neighborhood, declaring that these mysterious and evidently incomplete works were probably undertaken about the time of the Great Bfb, and may have been constructed by him in his (Herculean) attempt to subjugate the Massachusetts tribe of Indians."[27]

The Central held its annual meeting in Boston on October 29.   It was reported that "though little has been done in the way of road building... the affairs of the corporation are in a very prosperous condition." The treasurer's report stated that during the year ending September 30, $92,693 had been spent on construction, and other expenses had come to $219,675. $354,095 was still overdue on the Central's bond payments, while $31,468 worth of notes had been paid off or cancelled.   It was hoped that the line could be completed by November, 1880.[28]

The board of directors underwent a major reshuffling, as did the officers of the road.   Added to the board were Franklin Haven (one of Munson's assoiates), Josiah G. Abbott, Amos Stetson, and William T. Parker (all four from Boston), trustee Thomas Talbot (from Billerica), and Ginery Twichell of Brookline, who had resigned from the Boston & Albany RR board in 1877.   Oliver Ames, of Easton, who had served briefly as President of the Union Pacific RR, was elected to the board, but chose not to serve.   James Draper was dropped from the board, and replaced as Clerk by George F. Seymour, Silas's 35 year old son.

The most important addition to the board was George S. Boutwell, of Groton. Boutwell's name had appeared in Central affairs for the first time in the line's 1879 annual report to the state, as the Justice of the Peace before whom it was sworn for accuracy.   Silas Seymour had became involved with the Adirondack RR in upstate New York, and apparently preferred to concentrate on that project.   He retained his seat on the Central board, but was succeeded as President by George Boutwell.

Who was George Sewell Boutwell? Born in 1818, he was the son of a Brookline Mass. farmer, but grew up in Lunenburg, Mass. While still being educated in public schools, he worked in a local store. Moving to Groton, Mass., he married in 1841, and was elected to the first of seven terms to the state House of Representatives.

After failing in three tries for a seat in Congress, he was chosen sen as Governor by the legislature after a deadlocked election in 1850. He was re-elected for another year in that office.   From 1855-61 he served as the Secretary of the State Board of Education, during

George S. Boutwell
(Detail from F.P. Vinton painting
in Mass. State House)

which time he helped to build up the school systems of the state.[29]

When the U.S. Dept. of Internal Revenue was created in 1862 to collect taxes for financing the Civil War, President Lincoln named Boutwell the first Commissioner.   After getting the department up and running, Boutwell resigned eight months later to take a seat in Congress, which he held for six years.

In Congress, Boutwell was considered one of the "Radical" Republicans, and was a member of the Joint Committee on Reconstruction. On the positive side of this service, he is credited with helping to write the 14th Amendment to the Constitution, and advocating for passage of the 15th Amendment. On the negative side, Boutwell was a "fanatical" proponent of his party's reconstruction program, which led to his being named one of the seven "managers" of the impeachment proceedings against President Andrew Johnson.[30]

When U.S. Grant succeeded Johnson as President, Boutwell was rewarded for his party loyalty with the post of Secretary of the Treasury. In spite of his authorship of a book on federal taxes, Boutwell was not considered to be well-qualified for this post, and was an opponent of civil service reform. However, Boutwell did reduce the federal debt, and ended the attempt to corner the gold market in 1869 by releasing Treasury gold for sale.[31]

After leaving the Treasury post, Boutwell served four years as a U.S. Senator for Massachusetts. When he was not re-elected in 1876, he did legal work for the U.S. State Department. One newspaper, at the end of Boutwell's senate term, called him "a strictly moral and personally upright man himself, yet he is perfectly willing to use bad men... and to resort to questionable means of policy for the sake of maintaining the party in power."[32]   Boutwell would bring a nationally eminent name to the Central Presidency, although it would turn out that his knowledge of railroad operations was limited.

Two bits of good news for the Central came at the end of 1879. The state manager of the Hoosac Tunnel, in his annual report, "presumed" that the Central would be completed during the following year. However, S.D. Kendall, a Hardwick man who was the Central's chief surveyor, was "doubtful" that thw whole line would open "much before July, 1881," As it turned out, Kendall was only partially near the mark, but he was more realistic about the line's prospects than many other observers.[33]

A more beneficial event was an agreement to repurchase of the rest of the Central's outstanding bonds, at about 40% of their face value. These seven percent bonds were to be replaced by six percenters, up to the $3,500,000 deemed necessary to complete the road. A syndicate agreed to take $1,500,000 of the new bonds, and a committee consisting of Boutwell, Amos Stetson, and George Riley was appointed to handle the Central's affairs with them.

Negotiations with the Boston & Lowell RR for use of their line and facilities in Boston resulted in an agreement during the winter of 1880. The Central was to be leased by the Boston & Lowell, providing the line was completed by November, 1881. The lease was to run for 25 years, with the Boston & Lowell paying the Central 25% of the gross earnings. However, the Central would have to pay terminal charges of 30 to 50 cents a ton for freight carried over the Boston & Lowell. That railroad would pay all taxes of the Central, and supply it a Boston office. The agreement could be revised after five, or fifteen years into the lease.

This agreement was read by Boutwell at a stockholders meeting on March 13. 1880. Some stockholders questioned a provision allowing the Boston & Lowell to lay a second track along the Central. They were concerned that the Central might have to pay for it after the lease expired. When it was pointed out that

the   Central   would   not   be   obligated   for   the   track   (which   the   Boston   &   Lowell
would   have   to   remove),   the   lease   was   approved   unanimously.[34]

With   the   coming   of   spring,   more   work   got   underway   on   the   line.   Leavitt   &
Co.   were   given   a   contract   to   construct   a   bridge   over   the   crossing   of   the   Fitchburg   RR   at   Stony   Brook   in   Weston.   William   Flynn,   the   contractor   who   had   tack-
led   the   rock   cut   in   West   Berlin,   moved   west   along   the   route   to   Rutland,   where
he   began   work   on   the   more   difficult   cut   at   Charnock's   (or   Shannock's).   To   remove   the   estimated   12,000   cubic   yards   of   rock   here,   steam   drills   would   be   used.

In   May,   the   board   named   Silas   Seymour   to   the   new   position   of   Vice-President,
and   made   him   a   consulting   engineer.   This   move   was   reportedly   tied   in   with   Seymour's   connection   with   the   Adirondack   RR,   north   of   Saratoga,   NY.   That   line   was
building   toward   Ogdensburg,   NY,   where   it   could   connect   with   the   Grand   Trunk   RR.
The   Boston   &   Lowell   RR   saw   the   Central,   and   potential   connections   west   of   the
tunnel,   as   a   route   to   garner   western   traffic   via.   the   Grand   Trunk.[35]

The   Central   board   met   again   at   the   end   of   June,   and   voted   to   accept   the
route   surveyed   to   Ware   and   Bondsville.   It   did   this   in   spite   of   the   fact   that
the   several   miles   of   grading   done   on   the   old   route   had   cost   around $100,000,
plus   land   damages.   A   route   to   the   tunnel   line,   from   Amherst   to   West   Deerfield,
was   also   approved,   in   spite   of   the   fact   that   the   New   Haven   &   Northampton   RR   was
constructing   their   extension   parallel   to   the   same   route.   The   New   York   &   New
England   RR   was   reportedly   awaiting   the   opening   of   the   Central,   so   that   it   could
push   an   extension   of   its   Southbridge   Branch   to   meet   the   former,   thereby   gaining
access   to   traffic   from   the   Hoosac   Tunnel.[36]

In   July,   1880,   the   Boston   &   Albany   RR   bought   the   Springfield   &   NE   RR   for   a
little   less   than $450,000.   An   act   of   the   legislature   to   authorize   this   had   been
passed   earlier   in   the   year.   With   Chester   Chapin   of   the   Boston   &   Albany   one   of
the   principal   owners   of   the   line,   there   was   never   any   doubt   that   such   a   sale
(or   lease)   would   take   place.   Since   the   new   survey   of   the   Central   would   have   it
cross   the   Springfield   &   NE   in   Bondsville,   that   road   could   still   have   been   used
as   a   Central   connection   to   Springfield,   but   this   was   not   to   be.

Also   at   that   time,   the   Central   agreed   with   the   syndicate   marketing   their
bonds   that   the $1,500,000   worth   to   be   sold   would   be   at   80%   of   par,   with   an
additioonal   50%   value   in   stock   thrown   in.   The   syndicate   appointed   Amos   Stetson,   Charles   Sweet,   and   George   Riley   to   represent   them,   but   later   decided   to
hold   off   on   marketing   the   bonds.   This   was   done   because   bids   for   the   bonds   were
offered   at   95%   of   par   if   the   stock   offer   were   eliminated.   Sweet   would   be   involved   in   marketing   Central   securities   for   three   more   years.[37]

That   summer,   an   amusing,   incident   occurred   involving   three   Central   surveyors.   While   working   on   the   line   near   Wayland,   the   three   were   set   upon   by   two
large   snakes,   which   stood   up   and   hissed   at   them.   The   men   fled   the   scene,   with
the   snakes   following   close   behind.   Surveyor   Saltmarsh,   being   "more   heavily   en-
cumbered,"   noticed   the   snakes   gaining   on   him,   so   he   climbed   up   a   tree.   The
other   two   surveyors,   Patten   and   Hancox,   returned   with   sticks   to   fight   off   the
snakes.   Saltmarsh   "encouraged   them   by   his   earnest   prayers,"   when   they   simultan-
eously   rushed   the   snakes.   When   the   snake   carcasses   were   brought   into   town,   one
was   found   to   be   black,   five   and   a   half   feet   in   length,   eight   inches   in   circumference.   The   other   was   three   and   a   half   feet   long,   but   ten   inches   in   circumference.   The   newspaper   reporter   commented   that   this   was   "one   of   the   most   terrible
enemies   the   Central,   in   all   of   its   checkered   history,   has   ever   had   to   contend
against."[38]

Work   on   the   Central   around   Hudson   was   "pushed   with   great   vigor"   as   summer became autumn. Citizens of that town and Boylston "rejoiced" at this new activity. However it was predicted that the section east of Stony Brook would not be completed until the summer of 1881.[39] Contracts were awarded to Munson & Davis to grade the thirty mile stretch between Coldbrook and Amherst, while W. C. McClellan of Chicopee was contracted to do the grading between Amherst and Northampton. Since a large portion of the Central route east of Oakdale was ready for track laying, 4,000 tons of sixty pound rail was ordered in August to be shipped to sites there.

In early October, a "first spike" ceremony was held to note the laying of the first rail on the line. This was held at Snelling, where the Central crosed the Framingham & Lowell Branch of the Old Colony RR in Sudbury. Morman Munson drove in the first spike himself.

While Munson's act was encouraging, the deadline was approaching on the agreement made with stockholders involving the trustees. The Central's directors asked the towns to grant a year's extension on the time limit for the line's completion under the trusteeship. Only Hudson and West Boylston agreed to do this, but the latter town rescinded its vote a few weeks later. Therefore, Trustees Talbot and Haven returned the stock to the rightful municipal and private owners. If it accomplished nothing else, this maneuver had helped build confidence in the Central when it was trying to get back on its feet.

The 1880 annual meeting of the Central was held on October 27, in Boston. The treasurer repoorted that $487,546.47 had been expended on construction during the previous year, and that the bonded debt was $1,843,000. It was expected that the line would be open to Holden by February 1, 1881, and to Northampton within twelve months. The board of diretors was re-elected, with the addition of James Millege of Boston (who turned it down).

Track laying proceeded at a rate of about a quarter of a mile per day. Work trains were run to the ends of the completed sections. The first locomotive ever to appear in Wayland caused a great deal of excitement.[40] This was probably Munson's namesake locomotive, the *N.C. Munson*, which the contractor had used during his work on the Hoosac Tunnel track several years before.

Locomotive N.C. Munson, *just after making the first trip through the Hoosac Tunnel in February, 1875. Munson is standing in front of the cowcatcher.*
(Walter Fogg Photograph)

While grading work progressed in Waltham, a problem arose near the Lily Pond on the north side of town. The soil there was unstable, causing some of the grading to cave in around the beginning of December. Large rocks and whole trees were dumped into the foundation of the trackbed to solidify it, but a 150 foot section sank five to ten feet late that month. Much more stone and gravel had to be used to fill in the area.

As the year 1880 ended with active work on the Central route, 1881 was to be the highlight year in the history of the railroad. Construction would be pushed all along the route, with the eastern forty miles having track laid, and opened up for trains. Even though the corporation itself was stable, the work would be marked by accidents, strikes, and land disputes.

The first of two strikes on the Central that year began in early February, in Oakdale. The men doing the pick and shovel work had been given a pay cut from $1.25 per day to $1.10 when the short daylight hours in the late autumn had cut an hour's time from the work day. When daylight allowed ten hours work again, the contractor did not increase the pay back to the old rate. The men walked off the job on a Friday; surprisingly no "riotous demonstrations occurred" while they were idle. They returned to work on the following Tuesday, when the contractor assured them that their pay would be restored on March 1.[41]

A month later, men working for contractors Martin, Skinner, and Fay were told they would have to take a 15% pay cut to continue working. The men did not agree to this. One reason may have been because it was known that on a recent contract, this firm had paid their help with Mexican silver dollars, worth only 90 to 95 cents each.[42] It is not known who won this dispute, but the contractors may have just hired other men at their rate. When steam shovel operators on the Central line in Hudson tried to get a pay increase from $1.25 to $1.50 a day in April, the contractor turned them down. He anticipated having "no trouble in filling their places" with other willing workers.[43]

One can understand the reluctance of workmen to trust the contractors, when the failure of several of them to pay off laborers in 1873 is recalled. This occurred again in March, 1881, when the contractor on the Central route in Hadley "failed," leaving his men "out of work and out of their pay."[44]

Accidents continued to occur during the grading work, just as they had on the work a decade earlier. In mid-February, a cut was being made near the Whiting Mills in Oakdale. An embankment caved in, burying three workers. Oliver Kane was rescued alive, as he was only buried up to his neck. The other two men, one Kelley and Tim Niphen, suffocated before rescuers could reach them. Since neither of the dead men had any close friends among the laborers, the Selectmen had to take their remains to the town poor farm. One man's body was claimed by his friends; the other was presumably buried there.

Around the same time, a man fell off of some bridge staging near Boylston. He fell fifty-five feet, and "was taken up for dead." However, it was found that his "striking on an inclined plane," had knocked him out, and broken his arm in three places. It was reported that "others have had narrow escapes" on work sites in that section.[45]

Another accident occurred that February on the construction of the bridge over the Connecticut River. This involved the engine used to hoist the stone up onto the piers for the bridge. In spite of this, and the delay in delivering the stone from Northfield, work on the bridge piers continued. The most bizarre accident related to the Central at that time did not involve people. In the late spring, a violent thunderstorm hit Waltham. A lightning bolt struck a barn where contractor Dow kept a dozen horses. Three were killed outright, while a fourth was so severely injured it had to be shot.

Besides accidents, another kind of problem recurred on the Central. There had been difficulties with the grade settling in Waltham late in the previous year; another soft spot turned up in Hudson. This was at Scotia Swamp, where the railbed sank twice in March. The second time, it settled over five feet. Much fill was required to stabilize the grading there.

In spite of problems, the progress of work on the Central encouraged investors to have confidence in it. In late February, it was noted that the Central's securities had "considerably appreciated in value within the last few days." The company had just disposed of $500,000 in bonds at par, while "double that amount... could have easily been disposed of, one order for $100,000 worth from Connecticut being received... after they were all sold." This transaction left the Central with $1,500,000 in unissued bonds. Ironically, Central stock was not up to par; twenty five shares sold at auction in Boston a few weeks later brought only $23.00 a share (although some thought it was a "bogus sale.")[46]

Confidence in the Central was expressed by President Yeamans of the New Haven & Northampton RR. He offered to allow the Central to connect with his road in Northampton, and to double track his extension to the tunnel line if the Central wanted to take advantage of it. However, this would have been inconsistent with the terms of the Central's lease to the Boston & Lowell RR, so the offer was declined.[47]

The Central filed several bills with the legislature that winter. One was to extend its completion time another two years, to 1883. Another was to allow it to shift a portion of the Fitchburg RR in Belmont slightly to the south to enable the Central to use the route. A third was to allow the Central to shift portions of the Ware River and New London & Northern RR's so that it could run parallel to them. All three of these requests were granted.

Since the work on the Central was progressing at an uneven pace, negotiations were undertaken with the Boston & Lowell RR to alter the lease arrangement. Under the lease, the Central was to be completed before the Boston & Lowell would equip and operate it. Since it appeared that the eastern end of the Central would see its trackwork completed later that year, the Boston & Lowell was asked to operate that portion while the rest was under construction. Since the Boston & Lowell was expanding its terminal facilities in Boston for northern connections, this became a more viable possibility.[48]

Work on grading in Ware and Belchertown commenced in April, which scotched any remaining speculation that the original route through West Hardwick would be used. Enos Parsons spent much time making property settlements in the western towns on the line. One reporter commented that Parsons' health was "much improved by the outdoor exercize."[49] Considering the greed of some of the property owners Parsons had to negotiate with, his health could well have been impaired.

In Hadley, it was reported that "the immediate sensation is the great rise in real estate, limited, however, to the right of way of the Mass. Central RR." Parsons had "no easy task" to get some landowners "to come down where he can talk with them." It was "the aim of some owners to ask several times the amount they expect to realize," but they often settled for as little as a quarter of that amount.[50] The ones who didn't usually had their demands scaled down by the county commissioners after a hearing.

Parsons had similar problems in Amherst. He was accused of being "pretty 'rathy' and *independent* when often a more genial temperment... would adjust matters satisfactorily."[51] However, he had to deal with some tough cases. When W.F. Williams asked for $2,500 for land damages from the Central, Parsons told him that he "never attempted to meet a man 2,500 feet up in a balloon."[52] Williams was awarded $500 by the county commissioners. Other property owners in that town were awarded one quarter to one half of what they asked for.

That spring, the Central directors apparently tried to reclaim the three-quarters of the shares subscribed for, which had been given back to the owners by the trustees when the line was not completed in 1880. The stock was to be held until January 1, 1883. If the line was not completed them, the stock would be returned. Otherwise, the trustees could turn them over to whomever they designated, reportedly to bondholders. While Amherst voted to follow this suggestion, no other town is recorded to have done so. It is not known why this scheme was attempted again, as the line's finances appeared to be sound; its bonds sold for one point under par in June.

The advance of the work on the eastern end of the line also meant the construction of depots along the route. Sixteen were contracted for between the jumpoff point on the Boston & Lowell in Cambridge, and Coldbrook in Oakham. These "unique" buildings were said to have been modeled after the Linden station on the Saugus Branch of the Eastern RR. The singular style, inside and outside the buildings, was to be of wood, "colored and painted so as to produce an artistic effect." There was to be no plastering on either the ceilings or walls. One "peculiar feature will be the octagon ticket office in the center, allowing free access to purchasers of tickets" from both the men's and ladies' rooms.[53] The first one, in Belmont, was completed in early June.

The Fitchburg and Mass. Central Depots in Waverley (in western Belmont)
This shows the proximity of the two lines in this town.

Norman Munson was active in watching over the progress of the Central. On July 4, he visited Hudson, travelling part of the way over the completed portion of the line. He and some companions dined at the Mansion House. Exactly thirty one years earlier, when Munson was a contractor on a branch of the Fitchburg RR, he had dined at the same place. Munson returned to the town later in the month, "to examine the progress of work," including the foundation for the depot that was under construction. Since there was some complaint locally about the nine grade crossings the line had in town, Munson may have looked into that as well.[54]

Late in July, Munson ordered four "elegant" passenger cars for the Central from a Delaware firm, at a cost of $4,000 each. These were reputed to be modeled on ones used by the Pennsylvania RR. Other passenger cars were being built by Oscar Bradley, of Worcester. Munson also arranged to erect a building in South Sudbury for the manufacture of freight and flat cars.

Work on the Central around Ware had become so intense by this time that a labor shortage ensued. Some farmers, who had not secured their help in advance, were left shorthanded during a busy season. The price of "good" farm laborers went up to $2.00 a day, plus room and board. The Central work did confer a benefit for some farmers in Hadley. They used the finished grade for the "con-venience" of a "middle way" for their teams or produce hauling.[55]

While some Hadley farmers found it convenient that work on finishing the Central "crawled along very slowly," some on that end of the route were very disappointed. Amherst and Northampton citizens felt that the same type of effort going into finishing the eastern section of the line should have been expended between their towns at the same time. The fact that the road bed was "practically graded" reinforced their view. The Central could have had that "end of the road earning them something."[56] As it turned out, they were right in more ways than one.

As the summer of 1881 wore on, the time for opening the eastern end of the Central was fast approaching. The Fitchburg RR moved its track slightly south in Belmont, so that the Central could utilize its former grade for a considerable distance. The Boston & Lowell RR agreed to have its locomotives haul Central rolling stock to its Boston terminal, although the Central would be operating its own line until completed. This change in the lease was ratified by the Boston & Lowell at a meeting on September 14.

Preparations for opening the Central were made in several ways. A Mass Central Express Co., based in Hudson, was set up to handle freight on the line. A number of employees were hired, but applicants continued to seek jobs on the Central until it opened. Norman Munson named himself the General Manager of the line. The superintendent was Elbridge G. Allen. Two experienced conductors were hired. One was Myron A. Munson (the contractor's younger brother), formerly of the Woonsocket Division of the New York and New England RR. The other was Charles E. Tuck, formerly of the Central New Jersey, Old Colony, and Long Branch RRs. Engineers hired were Ephraim Tyler, of Hudson, and one Harris of Fitchburg. J.H. Palmer was the General Freight Agent; Baggage masters were Willard E. Brigham of Hudson, and George Munger of Waltham. Myron F. Munson (the contractor's nephew) was appointed station agent at Hudson.

The depot in Hudson, nearing completion, was painted cream and olive, with drab shading by E.

The Mass. Central Depot in Hudson (1899)

Perry, of Cambridge. The Central's 4-4-0 type locomotives arrived from their various points of origin. Their names were: *Bay State, Wayland, Charles River*, and the contractor's *N.C. Munson*. #1 and #2 had been built by the Rogers Co. in 1873, for a mid-western railroad. They had been purchased by the Housatonic RR in 1880, then sold to the Central for $27,000 a year later. #3 and #4 were built for the Central by the Schenectedy Works, at a cost of $25,000 each. The *N.C. Munson* was built by Hinckley and Williams in 1867.[57]

Before the route could be polished off for inspection, a few loose ends had to be tidied up. One of these was a controversial grade crossing at Lyman Street in Waltham. Due to the nature of the location, it would be busy as a grade crossing, which is how the railroad wanted it. However, a number of people petitioned to force the railroad to build an overpass for the street. This overpass would have been an "unsightly and dangerous" narrow structure, and would have caused the removal of "a fine avenue of trees."[58]

308 citizens of Waltham, at a town meeting, unanimously voted to support a grade crossing. The county commissioners approved the crossing, so it was sent to the railroad commissioners. Central President Boutwell appeared at the hearing, and promised that with "Pawtucket gates and electric signals," it would be the "safest of all grade crossings."[59] The railroad commissioners gave their assent to this on September 13.

Waltham North Depot c. 1930
(William Monypeny Photograph; Harry A. Frye Collection)

The track on the Central between Hudson and Belmont was in sufficiently good shape by this time to allow it to undergo an official examination. This was required before any segment of railroad could be opened for traffic. On September 21, Locomotive #1, with a Bradley passenger car, carried a party of dignitaries on an inspection trip over the line. Besides the Railroad Commissioners, others making the trip included Boutwell, Silas Seymour, E.C. Allen, J.H. Palmer, Central Counsel Henry Hyde, several engineers, and a contractor or two.

The train left the Boston & Lowell station in Boston at 10:15AM, arrived in Hudson at 1:00PM, and returned to Boston at 3:00PM. After a "thorough examination of the bridges and crossings," the commissioners "expressed themselves highly satisfied with the condition of the roadbed and structure" of the Central.[60] This approval allowed the Central to anounce it would dedicate the line with a special train on October 1.

The initial timetable for the Central provided for four trains each way each day between Hudson and Boston. Four additional trains ran each day between Waltham and Boston. One round trip train would run on Sundays. A two story brick engine house, with coal sheds was under construction in Hudson. The turntable built there for the Central was "a most creditable piece of work," with a "remarkably perfect" mechanism."[61] The Central was ready to begin operations.

Gleasondale Depot in 1934 (Known as Rockbottom to the Mass. Central)
(William Monypeny Photo, Harry A. Frye Collection)

Chapter Six: A THIRD OF A RAILROAD

October 1, 1881 was one of the greatest days in the history of the town of Hudson, Massachusetts. On that day, an event that had been eagerly awaited for a dozen years finally came to pass. The inaugural passenger train ran on the first 28 mile segment of the Massachusetts Central Railroad.

At seven thirty that morning, Engineer Ephraim Taylor started Mass. Central Locomotive #1 on the first round trip from Hudson. The rest of the train consisted of five Boston & Lowell RR cars, a Mass. Central passenger coach, a combination car, and a milk car.

The conductor was Charles S. Tuck. Edwin S. Breed (formerly an engineer on the Revere Beach RR) was the fireman. Other members of the crew were Willard E. Brigham, baggage master; E.F. Wells and J.R. Nute, brakemen; and Charles F. Buzzell, special brakeman.

Weston Depot

The passengers setting off from Hudson included E.G. Allen, the Superinperintendent of the road. He was accompanied by 200 excursion ticket holders, plus invited guests. The train traveled its first eight miles eastward to South Sudbury in a timely twelve minutes. About fifty more people boarded the train at this stop. Thirty people boarded at the Tower Hill stop in Wayland, and fifty more got on at Wayland center depot. Thirty five more passengers boarded at Weston, fifty at Waltham, and twenty five at Waverly and Belmont.

Only one slight hitch occurred during this trip; the train was held up at North Avenue junction (east of Belmont) for several minutes to wait for trains on the Boston & Lowell main line and another one (which was behind time) on the Arlington Branch. Once these passed, the Central train resumed its journey over the Boston & Lowell tracks toward Boston.

At the Boston & Lowell station in the city, many dignitaries boarded he train for the return trip. Politicians in the group included Governor John D. Long, Boston Postmaster E.S. Tobey, Collector of the Port of Boston A.W. Beard, Railroad Commissioners Kingsley and Russell; House Speaker Charles Noyes and House Clerk George Marden; State Legislators S.N. Aldrich, L.Taylor, Brooks, Joseph Burnatt, James Ray, John Wiley, Harmon Hall, and Estes

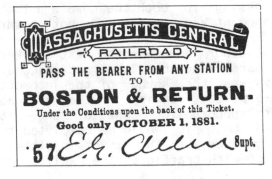

MASSACHUSETTS CENTRAL
RAILROAD
PASS THE BEARER FROM ANY STATION
TO
BOSTON & RETURN.
Under the Conditions upon the back of this Ticket.
Good only OCTOBER 1, 1881.
·57· *E.G. Allen* Supt.

Central first day trip ticket
(Wayland Historical Society)

Howe; and Councillor Hall.

Joining Superintendent Allen here were other officials of the Massachusetts Central RR. These were President George Boutwell, Vice-President Silas Seymour, Clerk George F. Seymour, contractor Norman C. Munson, and directors Luke Lyman and Charles Cutting. Other railroad dignitaries present included Adjutant General A.H. Berry, Superintendent Webber of the Northern Division of the Old Colony RR, Agent Palmer of the Fall River Line, Walter H. Jenney of the Chicago, Rock Island & Pacific RR, and Col. John H. George of the Boston & Lowell RR.

Wayland Depot

At 11:05AM, the train pulled out of the Boston & Lowell station to make its first run west to Hudson. Flags were waved at some of the stops along the way as the train passed through. A salute was fired from a cannon by H.B. Braman as the train passed by his home in Wayland.

Upon arriving in Hudson, the train was greeted by the Hudson Brass Band. One reporter described the passengers as they stepped off the train as "a fine looking body of men in their physical and intellectual development, and represented more avoirdupois, more brains, and more shekels than were ever imported into Hudson by the same number of individuals."[1]

James Joslin, Esq., and Col. W.E.C. Worcester escorted the procession to the Hudson town hall. Here, caterer George Patterson (of Boston) served up a "capital collation" of oysters, salads, cremes, and cakes, which was "utterly devoured" by the crowd.[2]

Joslin then called the group to order, and delivered a short speech of welcome from the Town of Hudson. He introduced George Boutwell, the first speaker. The railroad's President recounted the trials it had gone through over a dozen years to reach the point celebrated by this event. He noted that his association with the line had been brief, but that he had "always had a warm interest in its success." He saw the road as performing for the convenience of both local and through traffic, stressing the possibilities of the latter for trade with the West. Boutwell predicted that this and other lines with Western connections would need three or more tracks within 25 years. He declared the road a blessing to both the town and the state, and closed by invoking further encouragement and support from both toward its completion.[3]

Governor Long was the next speaker. His speech was "delightful," including a remark that that "the most welcome sound to the ears of the people of Hudson today was the sound of the locomotive whistle as it cheerfully announced the long-expected opening of the railroad."[4] He congratulated the townspeople on their support for "one of the vital institutions of the state." Long projected that it would be completed through to Northampton, then "creep through the gateway of the mountain [the Hoosac Tunnel]" to the Hudson River, to connect with traffic to the Pacific Ocean.[5]

Port Collector Beard spoke on the railroad as an important factor in the increasing development of Boston as a major port. Following Beard's speech, Governor Long rose to catch the 2:15 PN train back to Boston. Esquire Joslin tried to convince the crowd to stay for more speeches, including ones by House Speaker Noyes, and an historical address by Colonel George. Despite Joslin's pleas that another train would return to Boston later, much of the crowd followed the Governor in a rush toward the depot.

One prominent invitee who did not show up for the event was former Governor, Speaker of the U.S. House, and Civil War General Nathaniel Banks, of Waltham. When asked about Banks' absence, George Boutwell joked that Banks was in Washington "out helping [President] Arthur fix up his cabinet." A reporter speculated that Banks was more interested in keeping his "lucrative place" as a U.S. Sheriff than attending this event.[6]

Contractor Munson was quoted as saying that the line would be opened to Oakdale within another month. With that promise, what would prove to be the greatest day in the life of the Masachusetts Central Railroad came to an end.[7]

The Massachusetts Central was a fact. An incomplete railroad, but functioning, and rapidly finishing its next segment toward Oakdale. A 3,000 gallon watertower was erected in Hudson, and filled on October 8. The first eastbound freight on the Central from Hudson was eighteen cases of shoes from Francis Brigham's shoe company. There was some complaint that the passenger rates on the Central were a bit higher than those on the Fitchburg RR, but the Central's rates were cheaper if mileage tickets were purchased.[8]

Massachusetts Central Locomotive #4 at the Pope Street crossing in Hudson
(Walter Fogg Photograph)

With the opening of the Central to Hudson, the Charles Sweet Co., who was
handling the sale of the line's bonds, issued a prospectus. Demand for the Central's bonds had "practically ceased" after July 1, due to "the condition of
the market."[9]   This prospectus speculated that the Central would be open to
Coldbrook by January 1.   When the line was completed, it was projected that,
even if it did only half of the business per mile of the other major railroads
in the state, it would still earn enough money to pay off its bonds, plus a one
percent dividend to its stockholders. As good as all of that sounded, the prospectus didn't influence many people to invest in Central bonds.

Now that part of its route was in operation, the Central was the subject of
several proposals to connect with it. Marlboro, a few miles south of Hudson,
looked jealously upon the latter town's direct connection to Boston.[10] A seven
mile branch line from Marlboro to the Central at So. Sudbury was proposed, but
nothing happened. Another proposed connection was made by businessmen in Saxon-
ville, north of Framingham. Although they had been served by a branch of the
Boston & Albany RR since 1846, they may have wanted the direct connection to
lines north of Boston that the Central could provide. In spite of an offer to
contribute toward the cost, this project never got off the ground.[11] A third
idea was to connect the Central with the Ware River Branch of the Boston &
Albany RR in Barre. That line would be utilized to reach Ware. While this
proposal made sense from a practical standpoint, it had to wait five decades to
be carried out.

While work on the line was being finished up near Oakdale, more incidents
of drunkeness among the laborers occurred. Four laborers were arrested near
Hudson in the middle of October. A week later, it was noted that there was
"much complaint" in West Boylston that Central laborers "were bound to have a
drunken spree as often as liquor could be obtained." For "several nights"
during the two previous weeks. the region was "made hideous by their orgies."
This was blamed on too many local businesses selling liqour to the men.[12]

This problem also occurred in other sections of the route. Several laborers went from Gilbertville to Ware on a Saturday night in late October, got
drunk, and started fights. Only one was arrested; the others escaped. One laborer in Amherst wanted to sue a contractor for assault, but got drunk and passed out on the way to filing his suit. After being fined for public drunkenness, the laborer decided to drop his suit. Two other Amherst laborers had to
pay fines after going on a spree which included kicking a sheriff who was trying to subdue them.

When the Central's annual meeting was announced for October 26, stockholders
prepared to avail themselves of the usual privilege of riding the train to the
meeting for free. Those living west of Hudson had to go to that town to obtain
the free ride, causing one reporter to comment, "half a loaf is better than
none."[13]

The meeting itself was an anti-
climax to the opening of the line
a few weeks earlier. President
Boutwell did not attend, so Silas
Seymour presided. The treasurer's
report noted that over 90% of the
the $3,500,000 of stock was paid
up, and that over $2,500,000 in
bonds had been issued. Construction costs for the year ending
September 30 were $1,741,841. The

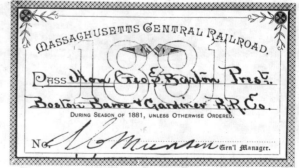

Mass. Central free ride pass for 1881

same directors and officers were re-elected for another year.

As work continued on the Central west of Hudson, a major obstacle was encountered at Steeple Hill, near Oakdale. A 250 foot long cut had to be made through earth that was "a very moist slippery blue clay." In digging through this, "the mud would slide down and fill up an excavation almost as soon as it was made." When the center of the cut was reached, a spring burst out a great flow of water, which was difficult to drain away. "Huge timbers" were sunk into the bed to stabilize it, but when a work train was to be run through it, a large slide had blocked the cut.[14] This was excavated, but another slide occurred a few days later, which tilted the track. The locomotve got through, but a boxcar was derailed. Piles had to be driven along the sides of the cut to shore it up.

Some obstacles, although temporary, were manmade. Two boys playing at the Central's gravel pit in Coolidgeville (near Hudson) got bold one day, and loosened the brakes on two gravel cars. The cars rolled down to the main line, which they blocked off. Apparently feeling guilty, the boys waited for a construction train to approach, and warned them about the two cars.

In spite of such problems, the section from Hudson to Oakdale was deemed sufficiently complete to have an inspection of it by mid-November. Besides the railroad commissioners, the usual cast of Central officials came to Hudson in a special train. After "they passed an hour discussing the menu at the Mansion House," they rode to Oakdale and back, then had a meal. The commissioners reportedly called this segment of the Central "the best constructed new road ever built in the state."[15]   However, they condemned a small stretch of track in West Boylston, so the opening of this segment was delayed.

The Central crossed the Worcester & Nashua RR at grade in Oakdale, forming a "diamond." A connecting track was laid on the north side of the Central. This would allow Central traffic an entrance into Worcester to the south, or Ayer and Fitchburg to the north. The connection was not convenient for trains going "headforemost into Worcester." This anomaly was explained by the rumor that the Central did not want to encourage traffic in that direction, because it was going to build a branch from West Berlin into Worcester.[16]   Of course, this never came to pass, but the diamond there would last for two decades.

While the Central was expanding westward, the line was adding equipment to its stock. By mid-November, it was using three of Munson's locomotives besides its own four, and had ten passenger, seventy freight, 200 coal, two express, and two milk cars (some of these were Munson's also). Business between Hudson and Boston was said to be "excellent," and most of the grading west to Northampton was being finished.[17]

Work to complete the Central continued as far west as Jefferson village, in Holden. At that point, the Central crossed over the Boston, Barre & Gardner RR. Central director Ginery Twichell had been a principal in the latter line from its early days. The Boston, Barre & Gardner reached Worcester ten miles south of this point, and ran north to Gardner and Winchendon. A connection between the two lines was built north of the Central.

The railroad commissioners, with Central officials, toured the segment in between Hudson and Jefferson on December 2, 1881. The commissioners found that the western part of this segment was "unfinished," so they did not approve it for traffic.[18]   On December 17, the commissioners again rode over this segment, and approved the use of the track. Although several of the depots were unfinished, the Central immediately set up a schedule of four trains each way per day from Jefferson. The trains were run to accomodate the the lines connecting at Jefferson and Oakdale.

At 6:50AM, on December 19, 1881, the first through train left Jefferson with 40 passengers in two cars. Sadly, the inaugural run was marred by a tragedy. Daniel Young, a 13 year old deaf boy, sat on the tracks near Oakdale to rest himself while on an errand. He never heard the approaching train, which struck him. He survived the accident for only a few hours. During the funeral procession for him the next day, a Central train passed by where the track paralled the route. This scared the horses drawing the pallbearers, causing them to be thrown onto the ground.

The Daniel Young tragedy wasn't the only bad accident to occur on the new railroad. On November 30, William Allen, a brakeman, was killed when he fell between the cars of a moving freight train in Waltham. A week later, four year old George Hunt had his leg cut off when he was run over while playing on a track in Hudson. On Christmas Eve, John Kelley, "while lying on the track at Waltham," was killed by a train.[19]

With the opening of the Central to Jefferson, a stage connection with Barre was advertised. This stage went from Barre to the Boston, Barre & Gardner RR at Hubbardston Station. From there the connection was made with a Central train to Boston. The whole trip took three hours and forty five minutes, and was offered twice each way each day for a total cost of $2.10.

Jefferson Depot

Around Christmas, track work west of Jefferson was suspended, although grading continued. A sufficient number of rails to complete the whole line had been delivered in Boston, at $62.50 a ton. The piers and abutments on the bridge over the Connecticut River were finished, and seven-eights of the right of way for the Amherst to West Deerfield extension was purchased. With all of this in readiness, it was expected that the road would be completed sometime in 1882.[20] However, new problems would arise to plague the now-operating Central.

As 1882 began, grading work on the Central was still being carried on around Ware. In mid-January, the work force was switched to the grade north of Ware, to try to speed up the time for opening the line to that town. A large stone bridge was being built to carry the Central over the Ware River in the southern part of Hardwick. The "crop of boulders" needed were gathered from the nearby Warner farm. Charles Warner was "considered especially fortunate in having such a substantial farm improvement gratuitously rendered."[21]

In February, there was one last proposal for a new connection with the Central. This was the old idea of a line from Southbridge to some point on the Central in Oakham, New Braintree, or Bondsville. The New York & New England RR was looking into this, but they could not "settle in their own minds" on which route to use.[22] The New York & New England was a financially weak railroad, so it is no surprise that the idea did not get beyond the talking stage. The part of this route between Southbridge and Palmer would be graded by the Grand Trunk RR three decades later, but not completed as a railroad.

A bit of good news for the Central came out of the Barre town meeting on March 6. It was voted to pay the balance due on the town's stock subscription, and a committe was appointed to negotiate the final figure with the Central. The town ended up giving the railroad $4,385.72 in cash, and $19,000 in notes in payment for the remainder of their stock subscription.

Barre's money would prove a mere drop in the bucket compared with the financial difficulties the Central faced that spring. The first signs of this appeared in April, at the worksites in Ware. Complaints were made that the day laborers were not being paid regularly for their work. The was an especial hardship, as these laborers were "mostly poor men and need their earnings."[23]

Later that month, it was noted that the full-time laborers in Ware had not been paid for the past three months. One of the sub-contractors tried to leave town without paying his men. They surrounded him, and "demanded their pay in a manner not to be misunderstood," so he complied. The reporter relating this incident observed that, while he opposed "lynch law," that "contractors on the Mass. Central have cheated the laborers about long enough, and if there is no law by which they can secure their pay, there might be some excuse if more forcible measures were adopted."[24] A week later, the same newspaper observed that "the Central does not show a great deal of life in this vicinity."[25]

It was unfortunate that the Central did not finish its trackwork at least as far as Coldbrook. That would have allowed the line to tap into traffic from Barre, Hardwick, and Ware, via. the Ware River RR. The additional income from such traffic might have made the Central's financial picture a bit less gloomy. The first ten months after it opened, the Central lost an average of $5,400 a month on its operations. In an attempt to garner more business, the Central added another train each way from Hudson to Boston in early May.

As it would turn out, the Central would need a lot more than an extra train to solve its financial problems, which took a turn for the worse that spring.

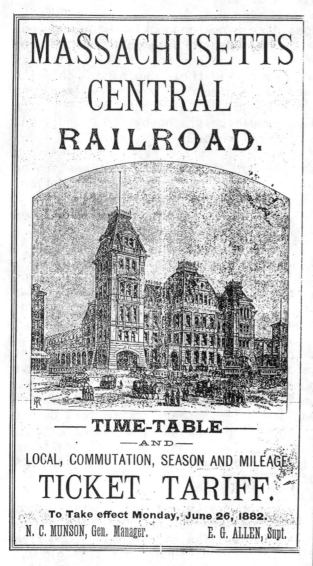

MASSACHUSETTS CENTRAL RAILROAD.

—TIME-TABLE—
—AND—
LOCAL, COMMUTATION, SEASON AND MILEAGE
TICKET TARIFF.
To Take effect Monday, June 26, 1882.
N. C. MUNSON, Gen. Manager.   E. G. ALLEN, Supt.

COMMUTATION AND SEASON TICKET RATES.

BETWEEN BOSTON AND	Trip Commutation Ticket	Season Ticket One Month	Season Ticket Two Months	Season Ticket Three Months	Schol'rs under 18 yrs Three Months	Educational over 18 yrs Three Months
BELMONT	5 for 50	6.00	9.00	12.00	6.00	7.80
WAVERLY	5 for 55	6.50	9.75	13.00	6.50	8.45
WALTHAM	5 for 75	7.00	10.50	14.00	7.00	9.10
WESTON	5 for 1.50	8.50	12.75	17.00	8.50	11.05
WAYLAND	5 for 2.00	10.00	15.00	20.00	10.00	13.00
COCHITUATE		12.00	18.00	24.00	12.00	15.60
S. SUDBURY	5 for 2.75	12.00	18.00	24.00	12.00	15.60
HUDSON	5 for 4.00	15.00	22.50	30.00	15.00	19.50
BERLIN		16.75	25.13	33.50	21.75	16.75
CLINTON		17.00	25.50	34.00	22.10	17.00

MILEAGE TICKET RATES AND CONDITIONS.

500 Miles, good until used, $11.25 { Good for the use of family of the purchaser when each member's name is placed on the ticket.

2,000 Miles, good for one year, $40, { Good for a firm to the extent of four, with travelling agent, each name to appear on the ticket.

Mass. Central Timetable, June 26, 1882
This illustrates the old Boston & Lowell Terminal on Causeway St. in Boston
(Richard Conard Collection)

EAST-BOUND TRAINS.

TRAINS WILL ONLY STOP WHERE TIME IS GIVEN BELOW.

Train Numbers.	2	4	6	8	10	12	102
STATIONS.							Sund'y
Leave	A. M.	A. M.	A. M.	A. M.	P. M.	P. M.	A. M.
Jefferson's..............		6 25	E9 00	11 35		5 20	7 15
Winchendon, via B.,B.&G.RR			7 43				
Gardner, " "			8 16				
Hubbardston, " "			J8 37				
Princeton, " "			G8 48				
WORCESTER {Union St'n via B.,B.&G.RR {Lincoln Sq			8 00			3 45	
			8 05			3 50	
Holden Junction......			9 01	†11 36		†5 21	
Quinapoxet		6 30	†9 05	†11 40		†5 25	7 20
WORCESTER {Union St'n via W.&N.RR {Lincoln Sq			7 30	11 15		5 00	7 00
			7 35	11 20		5 05	7 05
Oakdale		6 40	9 15	11 50		5 35	7 30
W. Boylston		6 44	†9 18	11 54		5 39	7 34
Boylston.............		6 50	9 24	12 00		5 45	7 40
S. Clinton		C6 54	C9 27	C12 04		C6 49	C7 44
Berlin		7 05	†9 37	12 16		6 00	7 55
Bolton							
Hudson..............	6 20	7 18	9 45	12 25	3 40	6 10	8 05
Rockbottom..........	†6 24	7 23		†12 29	†3 44	†6 17	8 09
White Pond..........							
Wayside Inn	†6 31	7 32		†12 36	†3 51	†6 24	8 16
S. Sudbury..........	6 36	7 39	9 59	12 41	3 56	6 28	8 21
Wayland............	A6 43	A7 48	A10 05	†12 50	†4 05	†6 36	†8 30
Tower Hill..........	†6 45	†7 50		†12 54	†4 09	†6 40	†8 34
Cherry Brook	†6 49	†7 54		†12 54	†4 09	6 40	†8 34
Weston.............	6 53	7 58	10 14	12 58	4 13	6 44	8 38
W. Waltham.........	†6 58	†8 03		†1 03	†4 18	†6 48	†8 43
Waltham............	7 00	8 05	10 20	1 05	4 20	6 50	8 45
Waverly............	7 05	8 11	10 25	1 11	4 26	6 56	8 51
Belmont............	7 09	8 14	10 28	1 14	4 29	6 59	8 54
N. Avenue..........	7 15	8 20		1 20	4 36	7 05	9 00
Elm Street.........	7 17	†8 22		1 22	†4 38	†7 07	†9 02
Somerville.........	†7 21	†8 25		†1 26	†4 41	†7 11	†9 06
Winter Hill........	†7 23	8 27		1 27	†4 43	†7 13	†9 08
E. Cambridge.......	7 26	8 30		1 30	4 46	7 16	9 10
Boston.............	7 31	8 35	10 45	1 35	4 50	7 20	9 15
Arrive..........	A. M.	A. M.	A. M.	P. M.	P. M.	P. M.	A. M.

† Flag Stations. { Passengers wishing to take a train, will please display the flag.
{ Passengers wishing to leave a train, will please notify the conductor.

A. A Coach connects from Cochituate.   *G.* A Coach connects from Mount Wachusett and Princeton Center.
C. A Coach connects from Clinton.
E. A Coach connects from Smithville, Coldbrook, West Rutland and Rutland.   *J.* A Coach connects from Barre.

WEST-BOUND TRAINS.

TRAINS WILL ONLY STOP WHERE TIME IS GIVEN BELOW.

Train Numbers.	1	3	5	7	9	11	101
STATIONS.							Sund'y
Leave	A. M.	A. M.	A. M.	P. M.	P. M.	P. M.	P. M.
Boston..............	7 00	9 15	11 45	2 35	5 05	6 20	4 45
E. Cambridge.......	7 05	9 20	11 50		5 10	6 25	4 50
Winter Hill........	†7 08	†9 23	11 53		†5 13	†6 28	†4 53
Somerville.........	†7 10	†9 25	†11 54		5 14	6 30	†4 55
Elm Street.........	†7 12	†9 27	11 57		†5 18	6 33	4 58
N. Avenue..........	7 16	9 30	12 00		5 20	6 35	5 00
Belmont............	7 22	9 36	12 06	2 52	5 26	6 41	5 06
Waverly............	7 25	9 39	12 09	2 55	5 29	6 44	5 09
Waltham............	7 31	9 45	12 15	3 00	5 35	6 51	5 15
W. Waltham.........	†7 33	†9 47	†12 17		†5 37	†6 53	†5 17
Weston.............	7 38	9 52	12 22	3 06	5 42	6 55	5 22
Cherry Brook	†7 43	†9 55	†12 25		†5 45	†7 01	†5 25
Tower Hill.........	†7 45	†9 59	†12 29		†5 49	†7 05	†5 29
Wayland............	B7 49	B10 02	B12 33	B3 15	B5 52	B7 08	B5 32
S. Sudbury.........	7 56	10 12	12 43	3 21	5 59	7 15	5 39
Wayside Inn........	†7 59	†10 16	12 49		6 04	†7 19	5 43
White Pond.........							
Rockbottom.........	†8 06	†10 23	12 54		†6 10	†7 26	†5 50
Hudson.............	8 11	10 27	1 05	3 35	6 15	7 30	5 55
Bolton.............							
Berlin.............	8 23		1 15	†3 43	6 23		6 05
S. Clinton.........	D8 32	D1 26	D8 53	D6 36			D6 16
Boylston...........	8 35		1 30	†3 56	6 40		6 20
W. Boylston........	8 42		1 36	†4 02	6 46		6 26
Oakdale............	8 43		1 40	4 05	6 50		6 30
WORCESTER {Lincoln Sq via W.&N.RR {Union St'n	9 25		2 10		7 25		6 55
	9 25		2 15		7 30		7 00
Quinapoxet	†8 56		1 50	†4 15	†7 09		6 40
Holden Junction....	9 02		†1 54	4 19	7 01		
WORCESTER {Lincoln Sq via B.,B.&G.RR {Union St'n	9 25		2 15				
	9 30		2 20				
Princeton, via B., B.&G.RR				H4 30	7 22		
Hubbardston, " "				K4 45	7 34		
Gardner, " "				5 00	7 55		
Winchendon, " "				5 26	8 25		
Jefferson's........	9 03		1 55	F4 20	7 05		6 45
Arrive..........	A. M.	A. M.	P. M.	P. M.	P. M.	P. M.	P. M.

† Flag Stations. { Passengers wishing to take a train, will please display the flag.
{ Passengers wishing to leave a train, will please notify the conductor.

B. A Coach connects for Cochituate.   *H.* A Coach connects for Princeton Center and Mount Wachusett.
D. A Coach connects for Clinton.
F. A Coach connects for Rutland, West Rutland, Coldbrook and Smithville.   *K.* A Coach connects for Barre.

Mr. Terry

Mass. Central Timetable, June 26, 1882 (Richard Conard Collection)

LOCAL TICKET RATES.

A Discount of Five (5) cents will be made from the Local Rates, when Tickets are purchased at Stations, or when Trains are taken at Stations where Tickets are not Sold.

Miles from Boston	STATIONS	BOSTON	E. CAMBRIDGE	WINTER HILL	SOMERVILLE	ELM STREET	N. AVENUE	HILL'S CROSSING	BELMONT	WAVERLY	CLEMATIS BROOK	WALTHAM	W. WALTHAM	WESTON	CHERRY BROOK	TOWER HILL	WAYLAND	E. SUDBURY	S. SUDBURY	WAYSIDE INN	WHITE POND	ROCKBOTTOM	HUDSON	BOLTON	BERLIN	W. BERLIN	S. CLINTON	BOYLSTON	W. BOYLSTON	OAKDALE	SPRINGDALE	QUINAPOXET	HOLDEN JUNCTION	JEFFERSON'S	Miles between Stations
	BOSTON							16	17	17	20	22	22	40	40	50	50	65	65	75	85	90	90	1 00	1 05	1 10	1 15	1 20	1 25	1 30	1 40	1 45	1 45	1 45	1
1	E. CAMBRIDGE							16	17	17	20	22	22	40	40	50	50	65	65	75	85	90	90	1 00	1 05	1 10	1 15	1 20	1 25	1 30	1 40	1 45	1 45	1 45	1
2	WINTER HILL							16	15	15	20	20	20	35	35	45	45	60	60	75	85	85	85	1 00	1 05	1 10	1 15	1 20	1 25	1 30	1 40	1 45	1 45	1 45	1
3	SOMERVILLE							16	17	17	20	22	22	40	40	50	50	65	65	75	85	90	90	1 00	1 05	1 10	1 15	1 20	1 25	1 30	1 40	1 45	1 45	1 45	1
4	ELM STREET							16	17	17	20	22	22	40	40	50	50	65	65	75	85	90	90	1 00	1 05	1 10	1 15	1 20	1 25	1 30	1 40	1 45	1 45	1 45	1
5	N. AVENUE							16	15	15	20	20	20	35	35	45	45	60	60	75	80	85	85	95	1 05	1 10	1 15	1 20	1 25	1 30	1 40	1 45	1 45	1 45	1
6	HILL'S CROSSING	16	16	16	16	16	16		10	13	15	18	18	30	30	45	45	60	60	70	80	85	85	95	1 00	1 05	1 10	1 15	1 20	1 25	1 30	1 40	1 40	1 40	1
7	BELMONT	17	17	17	17	17	15	10		10	13	15	15	30	30	40	40	55	55	65	70	80	80	90	1 00	1 05	1 10	1 15	1 20	1 25	1 30	1 40	1 40	1 40	1
8	WAVERLY	17	17	17	17	15	15	13	10		10	13	13	30	30	40	40	55	55	65	70	80	80	90	95	1 00	1 05	1 10	1 15	1 20	1 30	1 35	1 35	1 35	1
9	CLEMATIS BROOK	20	20	20	20	20	20	15	13	10		12	12	25	25	40	40	55	55	65	70	80	80	90	95	1 00	1 05	1 10	1 15	1 20	1 30	1 35	1 35	1 35	1
10	WALTHAM	22	22	22	22	20	20	18	15	13	12		10	20	20	30	35	45	45	55	65	70	70	80	85	90	95	1 00	1 05	1 10	1 20	1 25	1 25	1 25	1
11	W. WALTHAM	22	22	22	22	20	20	18	15	13	12	10		20	20	30	35	45	45	55	65	70	70	80	85	90	95	1 00	1 05	1 10	1 20	1 25	1 25	1 25	2
13	WESTON	40	40	40	40	35	35	30	30	30	25	20	20		15	20	20	35	35	50	55	65	65	75	80	85	90	95	1 00	1 05	1 15	1 20	1 20	1 20	2
14	CHERRY BROOK	40	40	40	40	35	35	30	30	30	25	20	20	15		20	20	35	35	50	55	65	65	75	80	85	90	95	1 00	1 05	1 15	1 20	1 20	1 20	2
16	TOWER HILL	50	50	50	50	45	45	45	40	40	40	30	30	20	20		15	30	30	40	50	55	55	65	70	75	80	85	90	95	1 00	1 05	1 05	1 05	1
17	WAYLAND	50	50	50	50	45	45	45	40	40	40	35	35	20	20	15		25	25	35	45	55	55	65	70	75	80	85	90	95	1 00	1 05	1 05	1 05	2
19	E. SUDBURY	65	65	65	65	60	60	60	55	55	55	45	45	35	35	30	25		20	35	40	45	45	55	65	65	70	75	85	90	95	1 05	1 05	1 05	2
20	S. SUDBURY	65	65	65	65	60	60	60	55	55	55	45	45	35	35	30	25	20		20	25	35	45	50	55	60	70	75	80	90	90	1 05	1 05	1 05	2
22	WAYSIDE INN	75	75	75	75	75	75	70	65	65	65	55	55	50	50	40	35	35	20		15	20	30	40	45	55	65	70	75	85	85	90	90	90	2
24	WHITE POND	85	85	85	85	80	80	80	70	70	70	65	65	55	55	50	40	40	25	15		15	20	30	40	45	50	55	65	70	75	85	85	85	2
26	ROCKBOTTOM	90	90	90	90	85	85	85	80	80	80	70	70	65	65	55	55	45	35	20	15		15	25	35	40	45	50	60	65	75	80	80	80	4
28	HUDSON	90	90	90	90	85	85	85	80	80	80	70	70	65	65	55	45	45	35	30	20	15		20	30	30	35	40	50	55	70	75	75	75	2
30	BOLTON	1 00	1 00	1 00	1 00	95	95	95	90	90	90	80	80	75	75	65	55	55	45	40	30	25	20		20	20	30	35	45	50	60	65	70	70	2
32	BERLIN	1 05	1 05	1 05	1 05	1 05	1 05	1 00	95	95	95	85	85	80	80	70	65	65	50	45	40	35	30	20		15	20	25	35	40	50	60	65	65	1
33	W. BERLIN	1 10	1 10	1 10	1 10	1 10	1 10	1 05	1 00	1 00	1 00	90	90	85	85	75	65	65	50	45	40	40	30	20	15		20	25	35	40	50	60	60	60	1
35	S. CLINTON	1 15	1 15	1 15	1 15	1 15	1 15	1 10	1 05	1 05	1 05	95	95	90	90	80	70	70	55	50	45	45	35	30	20	15		15	30	35	40	50	50	50	2
37	BOYLSTON	1 20	1 20	1 20	1 20	1 20	1 20	1 15	1 10	1 10	1 10	1 00	1 00	95	95	85	75	75	60	55	50	50	40	35	25	25	15		15	30	35	40	50	50	2
40	W. BOYLSTON	1 25	1 25	1 25	1 25	1 20	1 20	1 15	1 15	1 15	1 15	1 05	1 05	1 00	1 00	90	85	85	70	65	60	60	50	45	35	35	25	15		25	30	35	45	45	3
41	OAKDALE	1 30	1 30	1 30	1 30	1 30	1 30	1 25	1 20	1 20	1 20	1 10	1 10	1 05	1 05	95	90	90	75	70	65	65	55	50	40	40	30	25	15		15	25	30	30	1
43	SPRINGDALE	1 40	1 40	1 40	1 40	1 40	1 40	1 35	1 30	1 30	1 30	1 20	1 20	1 15	1 15	1 00	1 00	95	80	75	75	70	65	60	55	50	40	35	25	15		25	25	25	2
46	QUINAPOXET	1 40	1 40	1 40	1 40	1 40	1 40	1 35	1 35	1 35	1 25	1 25	1 20	1 20	1 05	1 05	1 05	90	85	80	75	70	65	60	60	50	45	30	20	25	25		10	20	3
47	HOLDEN JUNCT.	1 45	1 45	1 45	1 45	1 45	1 45	1 40	1 35	1 35	1 25	1 25	1 20	1 20	1 05	1 05	1 05	90	85	80	75	70	65	60	60	50	45	30	25	20		10		10	1
48	JEFFERSON'S	1 45	1 45	1 45	1 45	1 45	1 45	1 40	1 35	1 35	1 25	1 25	1 20	1 20	1 05	1 05	1 05	90	85	80	75	70	65	60	60	50	45	30	25	25	10	10			1

Children between the ages of five and twelve years, will be charged one-half of the Local Ticket Rates; under five years, free.

Mass. Central Timetable, June 26, 1882 (Richard Conard Collection)

Chapter Seven: THE END OF THE LINE

A preventable business failure in Boston triggered the Central's latest financial troubles. The firm of Charles A. Sweet & Co. was a State Street financial house, which handled the Central's bond sales. When sales of the bonds fell off by the summer of 1881, Sweet and others loaned money to the road as an advance on some of the bonds.[1] One morning in late April, a bank called in a loan of $300,000 made to the Sweet firm. Charles Sweet was sick that day, and his son out of town. The other principal of the firm, one Reilly, was "away on a drunk." The leaderless clerks didn't know how to raise the funds to pay the loan, so it went into default. This caused the Sweet firm to shut down. This failure could have been avoided, since Sweet ended up with $500,000 in assets, after the firm's debts were settled.[2]

Since the main backer of the Central's bonds was out of business, their price began to drop rapidly. At the beginning of May, the bonds, which had sold as high as 105, were pegged at 62, and the stock at twelve. By May 10, the bonds had dropped to 48, and the stock to 6 1/8. This caused the bondholders to panic, so they called a special meeting with the stockholders on May 11. President Boutwell found it convenient to be absent, so Silas Seymour chaired the meeting, which was well attended.

Henry Hyde, a bondholder, reported on the situation that had led to the meeting, including Sweet's downfall. He expressed optimism that the line, if finished, would turn a profit. However, Hyde estimated that another $1,000,000 would be needed to finish the Central. He made a motion to have a committee look into the Central's affairs and report its findings at a another meeting. While the committee was being appointed, Samuel N. Aldrich, a lawyer from Marlboro, spoke up. Aldrich represented several bondholders, whom he said would be willing to help raise the money needed. Aldrich stated that they desired "an immediate statement of the condition of the road." This remark "was received with applause."[3]

Five people were appointed to the investigating committee, including three major bondholders, Hyde, and director Luke Lyman. The committee was to have their report printed, and sent to all stock and bond holders before another meeting to be held within three weeks. As this meeting came to an end, Aldrich asked the directors if the Central's problems stemmed from its backing of Munson "as long as possible," and if it was "not in condition to do so any longer?" Others present desired a statement of the line's condition then and there. The answers to both questions were not forthcoming.[4]

Although two of its the members were unable to serve, the committee issued a four page report on May 29. This summarized the condition and financial state of the Central. The report noted that of the $3,500,000 bond issue, all but $250,000 had been taken up by the syndicate. They sold them for prices ranging from 80 to 105, netting the Central $3,025,775. Munson reecived $250,000 of the bonds, which he sold at the 80 level. One sixth of this money (a larger amount than anticiapted) had to be used to retire the old bonds, and another tenth of it to make payments on the current ones.

It appears that the Central's syndicate committee was only supposed to pay Munson as work was completed. However, they paid bills and estimates as these were presented. Land damages and rails cost much more than had been estimated, and the amount of the 1871-3 grading work that could be salvaged was much less than had been thought. The investigating committee felt that Munson "had not always excercized the best ecomony in doing the work," and that "under a more judicious and prudent management, the work might have been further advanced."

However, the investigators concluded that the Central "could not have been completed from the proceeds of the bonds."[5]

The report also noted that state taxes had not been paid by the Central, and that $59,000 of other bills were unpaid. One quarter of the steel rails delivered to the railroad were held under bond, subject to duties and charges. It was admitted that much of the line's rolling stock was owned by Munson, and that it was mortgaged to some of his creditors.

The investigators hired H. Bissell, Chief Engineer of the Eastern RR, to come up with an estimate of the cost of finishing the road. He came up with a figure of $595,000 to finish the Central to Northampton, and another $342,000 to build the extension to West Deerfield. These figures did not include stations or terminal facilities.

With these facts in mind, the investigating committee made several recommendations. One was to increase the capital stock by $1,000,000, partly to be used in exchange for unpaid bond coupons. An additional $1,000,000 in bonds were to be issued under a second mortgage. $800,000 more was to be raised by subscription to pay bond coupons due a month hence and to complete the road.

A new committee was recommended to secure the subscriptions, and to negotiate a settlement with Munson. The board of directors should be reorganized, and replace the lease to the Boston & Lowell RR with a terminal agreement. The final recommendation was to contract for completing the Central to Northampton, but put off the extension to the tunnel line "for future determination."[6]

This report was discussed at a meeting of the stock and bond holders on June 1. President Boutwell was on hand to chair this meeting. Henry Hyde delivered a long explanation of his committee's report. He emphasized that the requested change in the board of directors was to give "those who now own the road" (the bondholders) representation. He requested that each holder of bonds or stocks subscribe fifty dollars, which would raise enough to finish the Central as far as Ware, amd pay the state taxes due.

A "spirited discussion" followed this report, with several speakers "complaining of the way that money had been advanced to Munson." Boutwell was asked if Munson was supposed to be paid when the Central was complete, "and he hasn't done it?" Upon receiving a negative answer, the man replied, "Then this is a kind of funeral procession of Mr. Munson's." Boutwell blamed the high cost of the rails, work required above the estimates, and the failure of the Sweet Co., all of which prevented the work "from having gone through."[7]

After some further "animated discussion" about Munson's contract, S.N. Aldrich pointed out that the bondholders were not there to discuss "Mr. Munson's failings, and the suspension of Sweet and Co." He emphasized that "if the road is to be completed, the bondholders have got to do it."[8]

James T. Johnson, Munson's "legal advisor," stated that other railroads would offer more for the Central than the bondholders had put into it. He expressed "surprise that Munson has been able to do as well as he has done." This comment was greeted with "hisses" from the audience.[9] The report was accepted by those present, and they voted to create a new committee to arrange for completion of the Central.

A few days after the meeting, the *Boston Herald* ran a story blaming the Central's problems on Boutwell and the other directors, for not heeding warnings "against the very difficulties which have stranded the company." The story accused Munson of "controlling" the Central, even of "ousting" Stone, and "compelling... his own man" Silas Seymour to agree to the lease to the Boston & Lowell RR. This writer felt that the "most important question," which had been left out of the investigative report, was whether Munson was to be "allowed to continue to act as contractor in constructing or manager in operating the road?" This story concluded with the assertion that George Boutwell had submitted his resignation to the directors several weeks earlier.[10]

The attampt of the new committee to raise the needed funds by a subscription failed. As a result, a meeting of the directors was held on July 6. A new plan to raise funds was offered, which would have had the bondholders turn their securities over to trustees, and be given preferred stock in a reorganized corporation. This preferred stock would be given double voting power, and receive dividends before the common stock. A new bond issue of $1,500,000 would be floated to complete the line.

The bondholders met a few days later to consider these propositions. A new proposal was made to assess $350 for each bond, and give the owners $1,500 for each $1,000 in bonds they held. This proposal and the earlier ones were discussed, but the bondholders couldn't agree on which course to follow. They decided to ask the directors to give them more representation on the board. Since the July bond payment had not been made by the Central, it was subject to foreclosure proceedings by the end of the year. Due to the fact that this would have caused a shutdown of the line, most of the bondholders wanted to avoid that event, and reorganize the Central somehow.[11]

A day later, the directors met, and agreed to let some bondholders have seats on the board. Luke Lyman resigned, and George Boutwell resigned his seat and the Presidency, being replaced by Samuel N. Aldrich. Aldrich was born in Upton, Mass., in 1838. He was educated at Brown and Harvard Universities, and began a law practice in Marlboro in 1863. Aldrich opened a law office in Boston in 1874. He served his town as a Selectman, and was the head of a local bank. Aldrich was a State Senator in 1879-80, and had unsuccessfully run for Congress. "Well-spoken of as a railroad lawyer,"[12] Aldrich had once served as President of the Framingham & Lowell RR.

Samuel N. Aldrich
(Biographical History of Mass., Vol. II.)

Before Aldrich and the board could do anything to prevent it, much of the Central's rolling stock was reposessed by the American Car Co. on July 18. This had been Munson's equipment. The directors managed to borrow more rolling stock to keep the line running. The Worcester & Nashua RR reportedly expressed interest in operating the Central, but only if the directors could secure the remaining equipment.[13]

Bowing to the wishes of Aldrich and the bondholders, the board reorganized at a meeting on July 24. Longtime directors Franklin Bonney and Charles Cutting resigned, as did Silas Seymour, James Rollins, and William Dickinson. New directors elected were Elisha Converse (the Mayor of Malden), Henry Woods (of Boston, but a Barre native), and Boston bankers Moses Richardson, Lyman Hollingsworth, Charles McLean, William T. Parker, George Whitney (one of the trustees of the Charles Sweet estate) and Thomas H. Perkins. The only remaining members from the old board were Ginery Twichell, L.J. Dudley, Henry Hills, and J. Edwin Smith. George Seymour remained as Treasurer.

Rumors about various lines taking over the Central flew about as the directors tried to come up with a solution to the line's financial bind. Some ascribed the selection of Aldrich as president to the "influence of the Old Colony RR," while others saw the Worcester & Nashua, the Boston & Albany, or the Fitchburg RRs as potential buyers of the Central.[14] A Ware news correspondent reported that his townspeople "cared but little" who took control of the Central, or "whether the old bonds become preferred stock, or what is done, so long as the road once reaches this town."[15]

While no other railroad took over the Central, its directors could not agree on a course of action during that dry summer. The unfinished cuts and fills in Amherst were the subject of two jibes in the *Amherst Record*. One was contained in a lyrical description of the view from the top of the Amherst College tower. It referred to "one long white, burning mass of sand... lying like the bones of some huge reptile of other days, whitening in the sun."[16] The other article suggested turning "the ditch, termed by courtesy the Mass. Central, into a canal." This writer thought that it could connect with the Connecticut River to reinforce the town's water supply. He concluded, "By all means, let us make some use of the ditch, since we have got it - and paid for it."[17]

By the beginning of October, the directors were preparing a report to the bondholders. They had already advanced $15,000 to keep the Central operating, but "found the condition of affairs... to be very much worse than at first supposed."[18] In spite of the certification of the line from Boston to Hudson by the railroad commissioners, five bridges needed to be replaced, which would cost $100,000.

The Central's 1882 annual meeting was held on October 25. The treasurer's report showed that $1,255,435.74 had been spent on construction during the previous year, and another $100,000 for the equipment. The operations account showed an income of $83,083, three quarters of which was from passengers. The expenses were $127,432, resulting in a deficit of $44,348. However, during the last two months of the fiscal year, the income had come within a few hundred dollars of meeting the expenses. The only other income-producing item was the sale of 500 tons of the rails for $28,755.

Aldrich reported that the bondholders did not favor foreclosure, as "it meant serious loss to them." He admitted that "there would be no money in the road until it is completed to Northampton... which should be done, above all things" Aldrich thought that the first thing to do was to pay off the employees, "which could be accomplished very soon." One ominous statement was that "the directors believed it to be the best policy to keep the road in operation, even at a small loss, although stockholders should not be surprised at any time to hear that the road had been shut down."[19]

One stockholder made a suggestion which would have been considered heresy in the past. He thought that, as "a temporary expedient," the New London & Northern and Ware River RRs be used to form links to complete the Central. This suggestion was "favorably received, and due consideration was promised it." [20] Ironically, the Central didn't do this, but the Boston & Maine RR management would a half century later.

The meeting ended up authorizing the directors to appoint a committee with full power "to plan for the adjustment of the company's affairs."[21] This commit-

tee wasted little time in taking action. Two petitions were filed with the legislature on November 24, 1882, for consideration during the 1883 session. One
was to extend the time for completion of the road. and the other to re-
structure the corporation. This would be accomplished by forming a new corporation, with power to issue preferred and common stock, and first and second
mortgage bonds.

The other petition was to allow the Central to build a "branch or extension"
from Bondsville through Holyoke and Westfield to the New York border. This was
the old idea of a line to connect with the Poughkeepsie bridge route, to tap
coal traffic. "Prominent New York parties" were reportedly interested in this
project, ready to "put it through if in any way possible."[22]

In spite of its financial problems, and proposals to revamp it, the Central
still operated as 1882 came to an end. The line still posessed four locomotives (plus one of Munson's), along with seven passenger, seventy freight, and
two baggage cars. There were twenty three stations, and forty four miles of
track. Several trains still ran both ways each day over the route. However, it
would be a race to see whether new financing could be obtained for the Central
before it went broke.

In January, 1883, a sale of Central stock took place at 3 1/2 per share, an
all-time quoted low price. The directors were investigating the scheme to connect with the Poughkeepsie Bridge route, as President Aldrich reported that he
had "many letters favoring the plan."[23] Some felt that a combination of the
Central with another road (such as the Poughkeepsie, Hartford & Boston) might
give it more clout with investors in issuing securities. At a meeting on January 5, the directors learned that the opened part of the Central was "the poor-
est portion, as regards buisness offered." It was viewed as such a "short haul
for freight, that the percentage to the Boston & Lowell uses up a large part of
the receipts."[24]

The directors met again on January 20, and unanimously decided to issue a
circular to the stock and bond holders recommending a financial reorganization
of the Central. This circular, which appeared a week later, proposed to follow
the plan outlined in the legislation filed the previous autumn. This was to
create a new corporation, convert the existing bonds to preferred stock, and
issue $2,000,000 in new bonds to pay off debts and finish the road.

In a preface to the proposal, Aldrich stated that the directors, after "care-
ful consideration" of the option of foreclosure, felt that such action would
"excite litigation" by the stockholding towns, which would cause "such a delay
and expense as would result in a large waste of the property, and great damage
to all interests concerned." Aldrich also noted that "the directors have the assurance that a new issue of the first mortgage bonds of the character and
amount contemplated, will command a ready sale." With the railroad completed,
the preferred stock would "have a large and increasing value."[25]

This document included an agreement to be signed by the bondholders, which
called for them to deposit their securities with the New England Trust Co., of
Boston, by March 1, and be given a receipt in return. When legislative authorization for the company's reorganiozation was obtained, the receipts could be exchanged for preferred stock, on a basis of ten $100 shares for each bond, and
one share for each unpaid coupon. This stock would have full voting power until it received two eight percent dividends in one year, after which the common
stock would receive any remaining dividends. The final provision of this set up
a managing committee, consisting of Aldrich, Henry Woods, and Thomas Perkins,
with full power of attorney for the company. All this was not to be binding

until at least three-quarters of the bonds had been deposited with the bank.

The circular excited some concern on the part of stockholders, who feared being "frozen out" if a foreclosure sale of the Central was necessary. It was pointed out that, under the proposed legislation, common stock in the old company would be exchanged for equal amounts of some in the new one, the only difference being that it would lose its voting power until the preferred stock got its dividends.[26]

A week before the deadline set by the circular, it was reported that fewer than one quarter of the bonds had been deposited with the bank. $100,000 in bonds held by the New York Astors were being forwarded. The trustees of the Sweet Co. were trying to get approval to deposit $300,000 of the bonds they held. Since it did not appear likely that all of the bonds would be turned in by the new deadline of April 1, the possibility of holding a foreclosure sale was discussed. This was considered the only way that the new company could get clear title to the property.[27]

By the time a stockholders meeting was held on March 17, the bank had received pledges or deposited bonds from nearly two-thirds of the bondholders. At this meeting, it was voted to ratify all previously issued bonds and notes of the company, even those "not approved and certified" by "some persons appointed by the corporation for that purpose."[28] This was done to assure the legislature that the reorganized corporation would honor all of its obligations.

A large bondholder, Loring of Boston, wanted an investigation of the bonds issued in 1882, their legality, and what became of the proceeds from them. After "considerable discussion... regarding the desirability of investigating... the conduct of the old board of directors," the matter was tabled, with the understanding that it would be looked into. Aldrich stated that the Central was operating "at a great loss," but that it was "deemed wise to incur the lesser loss of keeping the road in operation" rather than shutting it down.[29] The meeting ended with a vote indorsing the current directors.

A few days later, on March 23, the legislation to reorganize the Central was signed by Governor Benjamin Butler. This allowed a month for all of the outstanding bonds to be deposited with the bank, or foreclosure proceedings would have to be initiated. The passage of the reorganization bill boosted the value of Central stock, as five shares sold a few days later for 8 1/2, which was five points higher than the last known sale.

It was at this time that Norman Munson makes a last appearance in the story of the Central. In March, 1883, he was reportedly interested in reviving the old Lancaster & Hudson RR, and connecting it with the Central. This would have allowed express trains to run from Clinton to Boston. The eight mile long Lancaster & Hudson RR was built in the early 1870s to connect its namesake towns. It was to have been run by the Worcester & Nashua and the Fitchburg RRs, but a lawsuit by a disgruntled abutter may have scared off the suitors, as the line never ran a revenue train. The tracks were still in place, although "covered with brush and grass in some places."[30] Nothing came of this scheme, and the Lancaster & Hudson RR was sold off at a foreclosure auction later that year. The tracks were removed, and the little line passed into history.

When the April 23 deadline arrived, almost $3,000,000 of the Central's bonds had been deposited with the bank, but over $500,000 worth were still not accounted for. The bonds were quoted on the market at a lowly 40 3/4. Some of the bondholders were reportedly holding out because they were "of the opinion that foreclosure was desirable,"[31] In anticipation of the holdouts,

Thomas Talbot
(From a painting at the Mass. State House)

President Aldrich had is-
sued another circular to
the bondholders to seek
their spproval to turn the
Central over to three trustees. One of them was former Governor Thomas Talbot,
who had served as a trustee
for the Central three years
earlier. The other two were
Franklin Haven (also a previous Central trustee) and
George Chapman, respective-
ly President and Cashier
of the Merchants Bank of
Boston.   A majority of the
bondholders assented to this plan, so arrangements were made to turn the
Central over to them, so that they could advertise a foreclosure sale.

There was a delay in getting the Central turned over to the trustees. This
was caused by a number of problems cropping up with keeping the line running.
Negotiations were carried on with the Boston & Lowell RR to opeate the Central
until it could be reorganized. When officials of that line inspected the Central on April 24, they made a "very unfavorable" report on the condition of it.
This caused the Boston & Lowell directors to demand a "heavy guarantee" of
around $75,000 to indemnify them against damages.[32] If the Central could have
raised only part of that sum, they could have continued to operate the line
with the current work force, so this was refused. Inquiries were made to the
Worcester & Nashua RR to see if they would run the Central, but that line did
not express interest.[33]

The state railroad commissioners, hearing of the Boston & Lowell's skepticism of the Central's condition, rode over the latter line on April 29. The
fact that they made the return trip at an average speed of 45 miles per hour indicated that they "found the road in pretty good condition."[34] This must have
caused the Boston & Lowell RR to relent on its guarantee demand, as they agreed
to run the Central for the trustees, when they took posession of it.

On May 4, 1883, a special train rode from Boston to the eastern terminus of
the Central in West Cambridge. The passengers included Central trustees Talbot,
Haven, and Chapman, along with counsel Solomon Lincoln and President Aldrich.
The trustees had come to to take formal posession of the road.

The Boston & Lowell RR took over the operation of the Central the following
day. They retained the train schedule, but fired most of the management, except
for Superintendent Allen. President Aldrich tried to keep the Central organization together, and stated that, if he continued as head of it, he would be
"glad to give every man his former position." It was not considered likely
that the more experienced railroad men would wait for this to happen.[35]

The trustees filed a petition with the state Supreme Court to allow them to
raise $30,000 to pay for current expenses and to repair rolling stock. Any
notes issued to fund this would be a prior lien on the Central. The petition
also asked for confirmation of the operating agreement with the Boston & Lowell
RR, and to authorize the advertisement of the foreclosure sale.

While the petition was pending, the Central's troubles continued. Charles
Robinson of Hudson had an attachment placed on 37 pairs of Central car wheels

at the repair shops in South Sudbury on May 6. This was to settle a claim of over $1,000 against Superintendent E.G. Allen. On the other hand, the New York Assembly passed a bill to authorize the Poughkeepsie, Hartford & Boston RR to consolidate with the Central, if the two lines chose to do so. Since that line was also financially weak, this action would prove to be too little, and too late for the Central.

On May 14, Justice Oliver Wendell Holmes, Jr., of the state Supreme Court, dismissed the petition of the Central trustees. The trustees felt that the jig was up for the Central, so that day, they issued a notice to close the Central after the last train on May 16. The trustees stated that they had not "been provided with the means necessary to operate [the Central]. They have not felt warranted in raising such means by a charge upon property, unless by authority of the Supreme Court, and this authority they have been unable to obtain."[36] All three trustees signed the notice.

President Aldrich and some of the directors tried to dissuade the trustees from closing the road on the 16th. They wanted the trustees to "take the responsibility of continuing to operate the road" for a short time longer.[37] Some of the bondholders made "threats" to the trustees that they would be "made responsible for losses resulting from closing the line."[38]

None of these efforts changed the trustees' minds, even though their action was "severely criticized." One newspaper commented that shutting down the Central was the "only safe course open to them as conservative men of large experience," although it wistfully added, "No doubt younger men, with less fear of trouble or failure, would have pushed ahead and left no stone uncovered to put the thing through until solid ground was reached under a new organization."[39]

On May 16, a reporter visited the Waltham North station on the Central. He found agent John Trefry and telegraph operator Miss. Sanborn "preparing to vacate the positions they have so faithfully filled." The reporter felt that it was "most unfortunate that at the opening of the most favorable season operations should be so suddenly suspended." He observed that season ticket holders "would lose much by the suspension," and that guards would be needed to protect the Central's property in town. The reporter concluded with the speculation that the "palatial Hammond Street depot will doubtless be utilized as a henhouse during the summer season."[40]

As promiseed, the Central shut down at midnight on May 16. All employeyss were let go, except for a few watchmen. The Boston & Lowell RR ran a car over the Central the following day, to pay the employees for the two weeks they had worked under that company. Reportedly, the employees were "still waiting" for "several months wages" from the Central. Passengers and shippers were not the only ones "seriously inconvenienced" by this closing.[41]

As one newspaper noted, "the brief, but eventful career" of the Central had ceased. Prophetically, this writer thought that the trains would not run again "for many months," and that the closing "was a serious blow to the future prosperity of the road." He contended that, "It is not a great surprise to those who have watched the career of the road from the start." In summarizing the Central's problems, he laid the blame on "so many changes from the original plan, so many errors to be corrected at great expense, so many different parties in control of its interests, that the enterprise has suffered from its very inception. "Want of funds has been its great trouble," he continued, blaming that on "the want of confidence in the way the affairs of the road have been conducted."[42]

The *Boston Advertiser* commented, "whether it will ever be operated again or not is a matter of doubt... none of its promise has been fulfilled." After summarizing the history of the road, it delivered a harsher judgement: "there was no fresh moral to be drawn" from the Central's demise, but its experience should teach investors "caution in such matters in a very emphatic way... as a local road, it was not needed... and the cost of construction was excessively great." [43]

Even though the Central ceased operating, the corporation continued its efforts to reorganize. The directors voted to extend the time limit for depositing Central bonds until June 17, in the hopes of obtaining them all in time to forstall the foreclosure sale. Engineers were also hired to resurvey the proposed extension from Bondsville to the New York border, in an effort to determine the cost of this venture before the foreclosure sale was held. On May 19, the Supreme Court granted permission to the Central trustees to advertise a foreclosure sale, which could not legally take place until September.

Two months passed with little action regarding the Central. The deadline for depositing the bonds was extended again, to August 1, but some bondholders could not be located. That summer, it was noted that the Central's default was one of a dozen that had occurred with American railroad bonds during the past three years. However, these defaults represented only a small percentage of the bonds on the market.

The foreclosure sale by auction of the Central was held on September 1, in Hudson. The event was well attended, including some of the directors and stockholders. Only two people bid on the property. One of the directors, Charles McLean, of Boston, bid against President Aldrich, who was representing the bondholders. Aldrich's winning bid was $500,000, nine-tenths of which would go back to the bondholders he bid for. He told an interviewer that the railroad "would not be reopened until it can be placed on a good, firm, solid basis." [44]

On September 12, the Central's rolling stock was sold at another auction, also held in Hudson. Lewis Bird & Co. were the auctioneers. Accompanying them to the auction in a special car were U. S. Senator James Camden of Virginia, the President of the Knox & Lincoln RR, the general manager of the Boston & Lowell RR, car builder Osgood Bradley, Henry Hyde (and several other Boston bankers), Norman Munson, and other railroad men. The auction included four locomotives, five passenger cars, forty five box cars, twenty five platform cars, four baggage combination cars, two milk cars, and two snow plows.

Two of the locomotives (#1-2) went to the St. Johnsbury & Champlain RR, while the Boston & Lowell bought the other two (#3-4). The latter two would be renamed the *Woburn* and the *Marlboro*, and would survive until after World War I. [45] Some of the other stock was purchased by Senator Camden for his line, the Ohio River RR, which now employed former Central Superintendent E.G. Allen. The total amount realized from the sale was $60,000. [46]

The Massachusetts Central held its last annual meeting under that name in early November. Since the offices of the line were still at the Boston & Lowell depot in Boston, that was the meetingplace. The only notable change in the board of diretors during the year had been the replacement of Luke Lyman of Northampton (who had resigned in the spring) by William Gaylord of the same town. It was reported that during the last seven months of operation, the expenses of the Central had exceeded the income by about twenty percent. The stockholders authorized the directors to carry out the reorganization of the corporation, which would be done the following week.

On November 10, "a full representation of the bondholders" met again in Room 12 of the Boston & Lowell depot in Boston. Thomas Perkins moved that the new corporation, the Central Massachusetts RR, be capitalized at the amount of the old stock, and all outstanding bonds and unpaid coupons. After this was accepted, Moses Richardson proposed a set of by-laws, which were adopted.[47] The same board of directors was chosen, with two additions. William Mixter, a wealthy Hardwick dairyman, filled the deceased Ginery Twichell's seat. Samuel Atherton, of Boston, replaced George Whitney.

This meeting marked the end of the Massachusetts Central Railroad, but it did not mean the end of the organization. As the Central Massachusetts Railroad, it would continue to be plagued by the same bad luck of the old corporation.

Chapter Eight: EPILOGUE

While the Central was now under a new name, this did not erase the problems of the old line. For one thing, the towns and other stockholders had to exchange their old stock for common shares in the new corporation. This was agreeable to most towns, but the issue caused controversy in Amherst. The town meeting held there on December 20 readily agreed to exchange the stock, and release the company from the obligation to build through Enfield and Greenwich. But when the company sought to have its Amherst depot more than the agreed upon half mile from the Amherst House, this was voted down.

It took until January, 1884 for the directors to settle with the trustees and the court to get full title to the property. New surveys were ordered of a route to connect the Central with Springfield, and to check over the existing route. However, the same old problem with obtaining financing arose. An attempt to get shareholders to subscribe for bonds drew little response. A scheme to levy an assessment on shareholders to raise the needed funds was considered "wholly impractical" by the directors. Attempts to raise money in New York were unsuccessful.[1]

By 1885, the Central directors were casting about for someone to lease their line to. Offers were made to the Fitchburg and the Boston & Lowell RRs. The latter road agreed to negotiate with the Central, and in July an agreement was reached to have the Boston & Lowell refurbish the finished part of the Central, and operate it until a lease could be formalized.

The Central was reopened to Hudson on September 28, 1885. At points along the route, "large numbers of people were congregated, and liberal gifts of flowers, etc. tendered employees of the Boston & Lowell."[2] Service was extended to Jefferson on December 14. The old Central bad luck reasserted itself when a locomotive and two cars were derailed on partly flooded tracks near Waltham on February 13, 1886.

It took almost another year for the lease of the Central to the Boston & Lowell to be finalized. At separate meetings in Boston on November 6, 1886, the stockholders of both lines voted overwhlemingly to approve the lease. The Central was to turn over $2,000,000 in bonds to the Boston & Lowell for the latter to use to pay for completing the road. The Central would receive twenty percent of the gross earnings, with $100,000 deducted to meet the interest payments on the bonds.

Before much of the new work on the Central was completed, the Boston & Maine RR leased the whole Boston & Lowell system on April 1, 1887. This made the Central part of one of the largest rail systems in New England. Construction was pushed ahead, and the first train ran through to Northampton on December 8, 1887. Regular service commenced on the whole line eleven days later. It had been twenty years since the line had been first proposed, and eighteen since it had been chartered. The Central would henceforth be known as the Southern or Central Mass. Division (or Branch) of the Boston & Maine.

Neither James M. Stone nor Norman Munson lived to see the completion of the railroad they had put so much effort into.

Although his decade as President of the Mass. Central had not come to a satisfying conclusion, Stone still remained interested in railway projects. In April, 1879, he helped to organize the Ocean Terminal Railroad Co., a scheme to connect Chelsea and Boston.

Stone died a few days before Christmas in 1880, at the age of 63. The funeral, held in his home at 26 Green St. in Charlestown, was attended by many local dignitaries. One of the pallbearers, and the only Mass. Central personality reported at the funeral was Francis Parker. Stone was buried in Mt. Auburn Cemetery.

It can be safely asserted that the speakership of the Mass. House was the highlight of Stone's career. His efforts in heading up the renovation of the State House and running the Mass. Central RR seemed to reveal the flaws in his character. These included the assumption of responsibilities beyond his legal mandate, and a propensity to place concern with his salary above the best interests of the organization he was serving. While he demonstrated abilities as a promoter and lobbyist for the Mass. Central in its early years, he degenerated into a mere apologist for his own and other's errors a few years later.

Norman Munson continued to be involved in contracting work after the demise of the Mass. Central RR. A visitor to his Boston office in October, 1882 found his features "plain," and his form "stalwart."[3] Munson may have continued his interest in the Central, as he visited Barre a couple of months before his death. Munson died in his office, on May 16, 1885, at the age of 64. The reported cause of his death was angina pectoris. On the day of his funeral, business was suspended in Munson's hometown of Shirley, and church bells tolled in his honor.[4]

George Boutwell continued his career in public life after leaving the Presidency of the Central. He carried on a practice in international law, highlighted by serving on cases involving claims between American and French citizens. Ironically, he ended his career by withdrawing from the Republican Party in opposition to its expansionist foreign policy. Boutwell was one of the founders of the Anti-Imperialist league in 1898, serving as its President until his death in 1905, at the age of 87.

Boutwell wrote books on several subjects, including a two volume autobiography. Neither this, nor a 1989 biography of Boutwell mention his involvement with the Mass. Central. He may have correctly considered it a low point in his career.

Samuel N. Aldrich served a term in the Mass. House of Representatives in 1883, and was a director of the Boston & Maine RR. In 1887, he was appointed Assistant U.S. Treasurer at Boston. In 1890, he resigned this post to become President of the State National Bank in Boston. He died at his summer home in Lynn in 1908, at the age of 70.

Luke Lyman, the ostensible Northampton bridge builder, and later a Central director, resigned his position as Register of Probate in 1883. He moved from Northampton that year to accept a position as treasurer of the Dominion Bridge Co., of Montreal, Canada. Lyman was arranging to return to his home town when he died in 1889, at the age of 65. His involvement as a director and promoter of the Central was recalled upon his death, but not the payoff on the bridge contract.[5]

Longtime Central director L.J. Dudley was not present when the first train pulled into Northampton in 1887, but he did hear of it. He was almost blind, but served as President of the Clarke School for the Deaf, of which he was one of the founders. Dudley died in 1889, at the age of 74, and was remembered for his efforts on behalf of the Central.[6]

After the end of his career with the Central, James Draper retired to his farm in Wayland. He "conducted extensive investigations into the merits of Spiritualism," becoming "convinced of the truth of its most important claims."[7] He died in 1905, in his 94th year.

Francis Brigham, another longtime Central director, did not live to see the Central run trains to his hometown of Hudson. He passed away in 1880, at the age of 67. Hiram Wadsworth, a Central director for many years, also did not live to see the railroad come to his home town of Barre. He died at the age of 75 in 1883, a few weeks before the Central was shut down by the trustees.

What was the end result for the towns who had invested in Mass. Central stock? Even though the Central was operating again in late 1885, several of the towns felt that their common stock would never pay a dividend. The debt that many of them incurred to buy the stock (at $100 per share) was still a burden on their budgets. Selling it off for whatever it would bring seemed to be one way to raise a little money to ease this burden.

Northampton picked a bad time to sell off over half of its 3,000 shares in February, 1886. That city received an average of about $9.50 per share. Oakham did much worse when it sold most of its shares in March, 1887, receiving 20 to 27 1/2 cents per share. Amherst sold off its shares in lots between 1888 and the early 1890s. It received between $15.00 and $22.50 per share for its stock.

Hardwick waited until 1892 to sell its 112 shares, and was rewarded with a price of $20.00 each. Barre held its 900 shares until 1902, and got the most money back (on average) of these five towns, $21.00 a share. As an Oakham historian put it, that town's investment in the Central had not been "a total [loss], except from a fiscal point of view, for the railroad was no doubt a great convenience to the Oakham travelling public. Its operation brought some economic gains to the town."[8]

What of the Central railroad itself? In its first years, it was more important to the Boston & Maine RR as its only line located between the Fitchburg and Boston & Albany RRs. The Boston & Maine's addition of the Connecticut River RR in 1893 increased the usefulness of the Central. However, the leasing of the Fitchburg RR system by the Boston & Maine in 1900 reduced most of the Central to the status of a backwater branch. The underlying Central Mass. RR Corporation was bought out and dissolved by the Boston & Maine RR in 1902.

A seven mile stretch of the Central in Boylston and West Boylston had to be relocated in 1903 for the construction of Wachusett Reservoir. This brought the line within the borders of Clinton, and caused the construction of a tunnel and a viaduct bridge over the Nashua River. As part of this relocation, the Central utilized part of the route of the Worcester to Portland Div. east of Oakdale.

One moment of potential glory came for the Central in 1913. This was when the Hampden RR was completed between Springfield and the Central just east of Bondsville. This overcapitalized project was meant to connect the New Haven RR system with the Boston & Maine. However, the financial problems of both systems resulted in new managements, which did not want to pay for the unused line. This left the Hampden RR a rusting orphan.

Probably the most famous passenger to regularly ride the Central was Calvin Coolidge, the 30th President of the United States. As a State Representative, State Senator, Lt. Governor, and Governor, Coolidge rode the Central back and forth from his Northampton home to his duties in Boston. This ride is mentioned by Coolidge in his autobiography, and charmingly described by one of his major biographers.[9]

In 1932, the year before Coolidge died, through passenger service was ended on the Central. Three years later, the Boston & Maine RR agreed to sell 21 parcels of land in the Swift River Valley to the Water Commission building Quabbin Reservoir. These parcels, totalling around 70 acres, were the strips of land purchased for the abandoned Central right-of-way in Enfield, Greenwich, and Hardwick. The railroad received $2,500 for the land, most of which would be covered by the reservoir a few years later.

In 1938, all service on the Central branch between Wheelwright and Oakdale ended; the tracks were formally abandoned a year later. This turned the Central into two separate branches, with passenger service running only east from Clinton. The western branch utilized the tracks of the Ware River Branch of the Boston & Albany RR between Wheelwright and Ware, and those of the Central Vermont RR between Canal Junction in Belchertown and Norwottuck in Amherst. This allowed the B&M to abandon parallel Central trackage. A three mile portion of the Central's track between Hill Crossing in Cambridge and Clematis Brook in Waltham (which paralleled the old Fitchburg RR tracks) was abandoned in 1952. Five miles of track in Clinton and Berlin were abandoned in 1959.

While separate parts of the Central continued to be used into the 1970s, traffic slowly dwindled. Only one train a week ran over the western branch before it was given up in 1980 and 1983. The state purchased the right-of-way between Northampton and Amherst, including the bridge over the Connecticut River. A paved "rail trail" for bicyclers and hikers was opened there in 1993. Plans were made to extend this trail over the old Central right-of-way into Belchertown. The remaining eastern segments of the Central between Berlin and Clematis Brook were abandoned in 1980 and 1994. Thus ended the 125 year life (and eleven decades of operation) of the Central.

There has been some agitation to develop a rail trail out of portions of the Central right-of-way between Hudson and Waltham. In early 1996, a study was conducted by the Mass. Bay Transportation Authority to examine the feasibility of reconstructing the Central as a commuter line between Hudson and a connection to Boston. Like the original Mass. Central, this idea was pushed by a Wayland resident, Representative Hasty Evans. Also like the original railroad, this idea was seen as unrealistic by some. An editorial in the *Hudson Sun* pointed out that it "would cost many millions of dollars" to reconstruct the railroad, and it questioned "whether the service would ever break even." The editorial ended by applauding Evans for initiating the study, but it urged that the proposal "not be allowed to expand into building a rail system that would become yet another burden on us poor suffering taxpayers."[10]

The Massachusetts Central RR name was revived by a new short line, formed in the late 1970s. This railroad utilized the 25 mile long former Ware River RR track between Palmer and Barre. While much of this trackage parallels the old Central Mass. Division of the Boston & Maine RR, it does not actually follow the old Central route. Ironically, this Mass. Central had ideas of reaching the Connecticut River via. the old Central Mass. route, but it was not able to take over the tracks when the Boston & Maine gave them up in the early 1980s. The current Mass. Central conducts both freight and excursion passenger business.

In spite of its disappearance as an operating railroad, there are still many remnants of the original Mass. Central railbed to search for. Among the original stations on the eastern half of the line, the Waltham Highlands, Wayland, Cherry Brook (damaged), and Weston ones are still standing. Besides the aforementioned rail trail, a number of segments of the old rail bed are still visible along much of the route. The hiker or bicyclist who might wish to follow these segments of the Central is urged to check on whether the property is open to the public before going onto any of them.

For those who do not wish to physically explore the old railbed, but would like to see parts of it, a couple of stretches east of Clinton parallel state highways. U.S. Route 20 runs along parts of the old Central bed in Sudbury, Waltham, Wayland, and Weston. Mass. Route 62 parallels parts of the rail bed in Berlin and Hudson. State Route 122 in Oakham and Rutland crosses, and briefly runs parallel to a section of the Central bed.

Several segments of the Central rail bed in Oakham and West Rutland are on land owned by the Metropolitan District Commission. They can be reached from Route 122, northwest of Long Pond State Park. Much of the abandoned portion of the Central built through West Hardwick can still be found. High St., part of Upper Church St., and a private driveway in Gilbertville were built over the old unused Central bed. The largest continuous section of the unused portion of the Central in Hardwick crosses the Greenwich Road, not far south of M.D.C. Gate 43. This is a spectacular two-mile stretch of cuts and high fills, including the culvert pictured below. Some of this is on land of the New England Forestry Foundation.

Disjointed sections of the unfinished and unused Central cuts and fills can be found on M.D.C. Quabbin watershed land parallel to (and south of) the Gate 43A road. There is a gap in the bed where it crossed this road at a junction with the road to Gate 11A. West of this junction, the cuts and fills can be found running parallel to the north side of the road to Shaft 12. The further west one proceeds along the cuts and fills, the route parallels the shore of Quabbin Reservoir. The bed crosses a couple of old dirt roads, and passes by two interesting farm cellarholes. When it reaches the shore of the Quabbin, it forms a small peninsula, which juts out into a bay of the reservoir, east of the Baffle Dam.

Culvert on the unused Mass. Central bed in West Hardwick

It is interesting to speculate on what fate the towns of the Swift River valley would have had if the Mass. Central had been built through there. Would they have kept or attracted more industry and been more populous? Would there have been enough "life" in the valley to make it less viable as a reservoir site? It is doubtful that the Central would have made much difference for those valley towns, but we will never know the answer to these questions. Such speculations do make the Mass. Central story that much more fascinating to area history buffs.

Another subject for speculation is whether the Mass. Central could have been completed in the 1870s. Probably not, considering the extent of the scheme and the weak economy of the time. James M. Stone lost his enthusiasm and promotional drive when the line needed it the most, and Norman Munson was involved with too many projects (and had too many debts) to be able to concentrate on

finishing the Central.   Perhaps the Central might have succeeded with a connection to the Hoosac Tunnel, or to New York state, but its lackluster record
as a Boston & Maine branch shows that it might not have been very profitable on
its original route.

Thus ends the story of the Mass. Central.

SOURCES:

Newspapers Quoted (with abbreviations as used in footnotes):

Amherst Record (AR), Athol Transcript (AT), Barre Gazette (BG), Boston Advertiser (BA), Boston Herald (BH), Boston Journal (BJ), Boston Transcript (BT), Boston Traveller (BTv), Chicago Railway Review, Clinton Courant (CC), Charlestown News, Hampshire Gazette and Courier (HG), Hudson Pioneer (HP), Hudson Sun, Marlboro Times (MT), Palmer Journal (PJ), Railroad Gazette (RG), Springfield Republican (SR), Springfield Union (SU), Waltham Free Press (WF), Waltham Daily Tribune (WD), Waltham Sentinel (WS), Waltham Weekly Record, Worcester Gazette (WE), Worcester Spy (WSp).

Books and Pamphlets Cited:

Baker, George P.; *The Formation of the New England Railroad Systems*, Harvard University Press, Cambridge, Mass., 1937.

Boston & Maine RR Historical Society; *The Central Mass.*, n.p., 1975.

Brown, Dee; *Hear That Lonesome Whistle Blow*, Simon & Schuster, New York, 1977.

Coolidge, Calvin; *Autobiography of Calvin Coolidge*, Cosmopolitan Book Corp.,New York, 1929.

Emery, Helen Fitch, *The Puritan Village Evolves: A History of Wayland, MA.*, Wayland Historical Comm., 1981.

Harlow, Alvin; *Steelways of New England*, Creative Age Press, New York, 1946.

Hodgman, Edwin; *History of the Town of Westford*, Lowell, Mass., 1883.

Johnson, Allen (ed.); *Dictionary of American Biography*, Volume II., Scribners', New York, 1927.

Karr, Ronald Dale; *Lost Railroads of New England*, Branch Line Press, Pepperell, Mass., 1989.

Leyda, Jay; *Years and Hours of Emily Dickinson*, Yale Univ. Press., New Haven, CT, 1963.

[Lincoln, D.W.]; *Reply to the Charges Against the Boston & Albany RR, by a Vice-President of the Company*, Boston, Ma., 1876.

Mass. Central RR; *Mass. Central RR: A Brief Statement of its Present Condition and Future Prospects, Sept 3, 1879*, Thomas Groom, Boston, 1878.

Mass. Central RR; *Memorial of the Massachusetts Central Railroad to the General Court, March 12, 1879*, Thomas Groom, Boston, 1879.

Mass. Central RR; *Massachusetts Central Railroad, Prospectus, 1878*, n.p.,1878.

Mass. Central RR: *To the Stockholders and Bondholders of the Massachuetts Central Railroad Company*, May 29, 1882, n.p., Boston.

Mass. General Court; *Legislative Documents*, Boston, 1825, 1869, 1876.

Mass. General Court; *Acts and Resolves*, Boston, 1876.

Mass. Railroad Commission; *Annual Reports*, Boston, 1869-84.

Mass. Supreme Court: *Mass. Reports*, (Court cases) various years.

Munson, Myron A.; *The Munson Record, 1637-1887...*, New Haven, CT, 1895.

Myers, Gustavus; *History of the Great American Fortunes*, Modern Library, New York, 1936.

Paige, Lucius R.; *History of Hardwick, Mass., With A Genealogical Register*, Boston, 1883.

Rand, John C. (ed.); *One Thousand Representative Men of Massachusetts*, Boston, 1890;

Report... Upon the Alterations and Repairs Upon the State House, Mass. House Doc. #484, 1869.

Town of Barre; *A Memorial of the 100th Anniversary of the Incorporation of the Town of Barre, June 17, 1874*, John Wilson & Son, Cambridge, MA 1874.

White, William Allen; *A Puritan in Babylon*, MacMillan, New York, 1938.

Wright, Henry B.; *The Settlement and Story of Oakham, Mass.*, New Haven, CT, 1947.

Collections of Papers, Photos, etc. Cited:

Essex Institute, Salem, Mass.
Richard Conard Collection
Harry Frye Collection
Henry F. Hills papers, Amherst College Library Archives.
Massachusetts State Archives, Boston, Mass.
Swift River Valley Historical Society, New Salem, Mass.
Wayland, Mass. Historical Society.
Worcester County Commissioners, County engineering records, Worcester, Mass.

Other Sources:

Annual Town Reports, various years, Amherst, Barre, Hardwick, Oakham.
Commercial & Financial Chronicle (newspaper)
Eliot, Samuel A., (Ed.); *Biographical History of Massachuetts* (Vol. II), Mass.
    Biographical Society, Boston, 1909.
Hudson, Alfred S.; *Annals of Sudbury, Wayland, and Maynard, Middlesex County,*
    Mass., Boston, 1891.
Karr, Roanld Dale; *The Rail Lines of Southern New England*, Branch Line Press,
    Pepperell, Mass., 1995.
Marquis, A.N. Co.; *Who Was Who in America*, Volume I, Chicago, 1966
Mass. House and Senate, *Acts and Resolves*, various years, Boston.
Massachusetts State Library, Special Collections, Boston.
Metropolitan District Commission, Watershed Management Div., files, Quabbin Sec-
    tion.
Simonhoff, Harry; *Sketches of Men of Mark*, New York & Hartford Pub. Co., 1871.
Sweet, Charles A. & Co., *Massachusetts Central Railroad Co.* (Prospectus, 1881).

FOOTNOTES (Numbered by Chapter; newspaper abbreviations listed in Sources):

Chapter One: 1) Senate Doc. #5, 1825, pp. 12. 2) Ibid., p. 14. 3) Letter to Southworth at Swift River Valley Historical Society 4) SR 1/1/70. 5) John C. Rand (ed.), *One Thousand Representative Men,* p. 185. 6) BG 10/18/67. 7) HG 12/10/67. 8) HG 1/21/68, 7/25/71. 9) BG 10/23/68. 10) WS 10/23/68, WF 10/30/68, PJ 10/24/68. 11) BA 10/20/68. 12) HG 10/27/68. 13} AR 11/5/68, BG 11/13/68. 14) WSp 11/6/68. 15) HG 1/5/69. 16) BG 1/29/69. 17) BG 3/12/69. 18) BG 3/26/69. 19) AR 4/15/69. 20) SU 6/10/69. 21) SR 6/7/69. 22) SU 6/7/69. 23) BG 6/18/69. 24) 6/8/69. 25) SR 6/16 & 19/69. 26) SR 6/20/69.

Chapter Two: 1) *Charlestown News,* 12/25/80. 2) Edwin Hodgman, *History of the Town of Westford,* p. 345. 3) House Doc. #404, 1869. 4) SR 1/1/70. 5) SR 1/1/70. 6) House Doc. #355, 1876, Appendix, p. 177. 7) WF 1/7/70. 8) BJ, quoted in BG 3/4/70. 9) AR 3/3/70. 10) AR 3/4/70, HG 3/22/70. 11) HG 4/4/70. 12) Ibid. 13) Ibid. 14) AR 5/25/70. 15) AR 5/18/70. 16) AR 7/6/70. 17) CC quoted in BG 7/8/70. 18) AR 8/17 & 9/7/70. 19) AR 8/31/70. 20) AR 9/7/70, PJ 9/10/70. 21) Ibid. 22) AR 9/14 & 9/28/70, BG 9/14/70. 23) AR 9/21/70. 24) AR 9/28/70. 25) AR 10/5/70. 26) AR 10/5/70. 27) BJ, quoted in HG 11/21/71. 28) WF 10/14/70. 29) BT 10/26/70. 30) BJ, quoted in AR 11/2/70. 31) Ibid. 32) Ibid. 33) AR 11/2/70, BG 11/4/70, BT 10/26/70, BA quoted in HG 11/9/70. 34) AR 11/9/70, HG 11/27/70, PJ 11/12 & 12/17/78. 35) BT 11/8/70, HG 11/15/70. 36) PJ 12/3, 12/10/70. 37) PJ 12/3 & 12/17/70. 38) PJ 12/17/70. 39) WS 1/13/71, AR 1/18/71. 40) BG 2/10/71. 41) BG 3/10/71. 42) BA, quoted in BG 3/31/71. 43) Henry F. Hills papers, Amherst College. 44) HG 7/11/71. 45) Hills papers, op.cit. 46) HG 8/8/71. 47) AR 8/16/71, HG 8/22 & 9/12/71. 48) AR 8/16/71. 49) HG 9/12/71. 50) HG 9/12/71. 51) BG 10/13/71. 52) BG 11/10/71. 53) BG 11/3/70. 54) HG 3/1/76. 55) PJ 12/8/71. 56) BG 12/15, & 12/29/71. 57) HG 12/19/71. 58) HG 3/26/72.

Chapter Three: 1) AT 1/16/72. 2) BA quoted in HG 1/26/72. 3) Ibid. 4) AR 1/24/72. 5) HG 2/27/72, PJ 2/17/72. 6) PJ 3/9/72. 7) AR 2/7 & 2/14/72. 8) CC 3/23/72. 9) BG 8/2/72. 10) HG 5/7/72, PJ 4/26/72. 11) Handbill at the Essex Institute, 12) PJ quoted in BG 5/31/72, WS 7/26/72, PJ 7/27/72. 13) BG 6/21/72. 14) 1876 House Doc. #324, p.110. 15) Ibid., p.53. 16. Ibid., pp. 83, 84, 153. 17) Ibid., p. 77-9. 18) Ibid., pp. 113, 79, 115. 19. Ibid., pp. 79, 94. 20) Ibid., pp. 114, 116, 117. 75. 21) Ibid., pp. 71, 111, 112, 115. 22) House Doc. #355, 1876, pp. 5-6. 23) PJ 8/24 & 10/12/72. 24) CC 9/21/72. 25) BG 10/25/72. 26) CC 8/24, 10/26, BG 10/25/72. 27) BG 10/25/72. 28) AR 10/30/72. 29) AR 10/30 & 12/4/72. 30) Lucius Paige, *History of Hardwick, Mass.,* p. 157. 31) BG 11/8/72, 2/7/73. 32) AR 11/13/72, BG 11/15/72. 33) Ibid. 34) Ibid. 35) George P. Baker, *The Formation of the New England Railroad Systems,* pp. 187-9. 36) BA quoted in HG 12/31/72. 37) BG 1/31/73. 38) HG 3/4/73. 39) HG 1/6 & 3/26/74. 40) HG 3/18/73. 41) WS 4/18/73. 42) BG 3/17, 4/4/73. 43) HG 5/13/73. 44) BG 5/2, 5/30, 8/29, 9/14/73. 45) CC 3/29/73. 46) BG 11/7/73. 47) HG 7/8/73. 48) BG 6/14/78. 49) Dee Brown, *Hear That Lonesome Whistle Blow,* pp. 216-7. 50) BG 6/14/78. 51) Ibid.

Chapter Four: 1) RG 6/22/85, HG 11/18/73, Mass. Central *Brief Statement...,* 1879, p.9. 2) PJ 11/29/73. 3) HG 11/11 & 11/18/73. 4) Ibid. 5) Ibid. 6) HG 12/30/73. 7) HG 1/6/74. 8) Ibid. 9) House Doc. #355, 1876, Appendix, pp. 193, 197, 144. 10) SU 3/1/76. 11) House #355, q.v., p. 102. 12) *Reply to the Charges Against the Boston & Albany RR...,* p. 4. 13) House #355, q.v., p. 155. 14) Ibid., p. 262. 15) Ibid., p. 348. 16) *Reply to the Charges...* (q.v.), p. 5. 17) House #355, q.v., p. 199. 18) Ibid., p. 199. 19) HG 1/13/74. 20) HG 6/27/74. 21) Jay Leyda, *Years and Hours of Emily Dickinson,* p. 209. 22) HG 2/24/74. 23) SU, quoted in HG 3/24/74. 24) Ibid. 25) BG 5/29/74. 26) HG 6/23/74. 27) *One Hundredth Anniversary of... The Town of Barre,* p. 160. 28)

Footnotes, Chapter Four, Continued:

28) BG 7/10/74.   29) HG 78/28/74. 30) HG 8/11/74. 31) HG 10/13/74. 32) HG 11/17/74.   33) AR quoted in HG 12/22/74. 34) Karr, *Lost Railroads of New England*, p. 32.   35) Boston & Hingham Steamboat Co., vs. Norman C. Munson, 1875. 36) WSp 4/14/75.   37) AR 1/6 & 3/24/75.   38) HG 2/16 & 3/16/75. 39) RG 1/14/75.   40) HG 5/18/75.   41) SR 2/6/75. 42) Ibid. 43) HG 3/23 & 3/30/75. 44) BG 3/19/75. 45) HG 5/18/75. 46) BG 8/13/75. 47) SR 1/7/75, RG 8/7/75, BG 11/19/75, 1874 Mass. RR Comm. *Annual Report*. 48) BG 8/6/75. 49) SR quoted in RG 11/20/75.   50) HG 10/26/75, AR 10/27/75. 51) HG 11/8/75. 52) SR 11/19/75. 53) 1878 Mass. Central *Prospectus*, pp. 8-9. 54) WSp 1/12 & 1/20/76 (quoting SU).   55) BH, quoted in AR 2/2/76. 56) PJ 1/28/76. 57) HG 2/22/76. 58) SR 3/23/76.   59) AR 4/5/76.   60) AR 11/8/76. 61) HG 12/18/76. 62) HG 12/18/76. 63) HG 12/26/76.   64) BH, quoted in AT 1/26/77. 65) SR 1/27/77. 66) RG 3/2/77.   67) Alvin Harlow, *Steelways of New England*, pp. 255-56. 68) HG 6/19/77. 69) HG 6/26/77. 70) SR 7/6/77. 71) BTv, quoted in HG 7/3/77. 72) HG 8/2/71.   73) SR 11/3/77, HG 11/6/77. 74) HG Ibid. 75) HG 12/4/77. 76) BG 4/5/78.   77) BG 2/1/78. 78) BG 4/5/78. 79) Dee Brown, op. cit., pp. 57, 62, 108. 80) Ibid., pp. 59, 119, 70. 81) BG 4/5/78. 82) BG 4/5 & 4/12/78.

Chapter Five: 1) HG 11/12/78. 2) HG 6/25/78. 3) HG 11/12/78. 4) Ibid. 5) Ibid. 6) HG 11/5/78.   7) RG 12/27/78, SR 12/28/78. 8) WF 1/3/79. 9) BG 1/24/79.   10) BG 8/8/79, Mass. Central *Memorial...*, p.19. 11) *Memorial*, op. cit., pp. 11-12.   12) Ibid., pp.14-7. 13) Ibid. 14) Ibid, pp. 17, 20, State Archives file, Chapter 253, Acts of 1879. 15) RG. 4/11/79. 16) SR 5/5/79. 17) SR 11/24/79.   18) Gustavus Myers, *History of the Great American Fortunes*, p. 482. 19) *Brief Statement...* pp. 8-11 20) SR quoted in BG 1/14/80. 21) BTv quoted in BG 7/25/79. 22) BG 1/16/80. 23) BTv in BG 8/8/79. 24) BG 10/3/79. 25) 1/16/80.   26) BG 12/12 & 12/5/79. 27) BG 12/5/79. 28) BG 10/31/79, BT 10/31/79. 29) BG 3/19/69.   30) A. Johnson (ed.), *Dictionary of American Biography*, Vol. II, p. 489. 31) Ibid. 32) SR 1/27/77. 33) HG 1/17/80. 34) HG 3/23/80.   35) BG 5/14/80. 36) HG 7/8/80. 37) RG 8/13/80. 38) WF 8/6/80. 39) CC 8/14 & 8/31/80. 40) WF 12/3/80. 41) CC 2/12/81. 42) CC 3/12/81. 43) CC 4/9/81. 44) HG 3/8/81. 45) CC 4/9/81. 46) HG 2/22, 4/5, & 4/19/81, CC 4/2/81. 47) HG 2/22/81. 48) HG 3/13/81. 49) HG 4/19/81. 50) AR 5/11/81. 51) HG 6/7/81 52) HG 8/2/81. 53) HG 4/19/81. 54) CC 7/2/81, HP 7/23/81. 55) BG 7/15/81, HG 7/26/81, AR 8/3/81. 56) AR 8/3 & 7/27/81. 57) HP 8/27/81, *The Central Mass.*, p. 133., WF 9/30/81. 58) WF 9/16/81. 59) Ibid. 60) WF 9/23/81. 61) MT 10/6/81, HP 10/8/81.

Chapter Six: 1) HP 10/8/81. 2) MT 10/6/81. 3) Ibid. 4) Ibid. 5) BT 10/2/81. 6) MT 10/6/81. 7) BT 10/2/81. 8) HP 10/8 & 10/15/81. 9) *To the Stockholders* ... report, 5/29/82, p. 1. 10) MT 10/6/81. 11) RG 11/11/81. 12) CC 10/22 & 10/29/81. 13) CC 10/22/81. 14) CC 11/26/81. 15) HP 11/19/81. 16) HP 11/18/81. 17) PJ 11/19/81. 18) WE 12/16/81. 19) 1882 Mass. RR Comm *Annual Report*, p. 151. 20) BG 1/6/82. 21) BG 1/27/82. 22) PJ 2/18/82. 23) BG 4/7/82. 24) BG 4/28/82. 25) BG 5/5/82.

Chapter Seven: 1) BT 5/31/82. 2) PJ 3/25/87 & AR 3/16/87. 3) BT 5/11/82. 4) ibid. 5) *To the Stockholders...* report, 5/29/82, p. 2. 6) Ibid., p.3. 7) BT 6/1/82. 8) Ibid. 9) Ibid. 10) BH, quoted in BT 6/5/82. 11) RG 7/21/82. 12) AR 7/26/82. 13) RG 7/21/82. 14) AR 7/26/82. 15) PJ 7/22/82. 16) AR 8/16/82. 17) AR 8/23/82. 18) BG 10/6/82. 19) BG 10/27/82. 20) RG 10/27/82. 21) Ibid. 22) RG 12/1/82. 23) BG 1/19/83. 24) RG 1/12/83. 25) BG 2/2/83. 26) BG 3/2/83.   27) RG 3/16/83. 28) RG 3/23/83. 29) Ibid. 30) BG 3/23/83. 31) BT 4/19/83.   32) BT 4/25&26/83. 33) 4/30/83. 34) BG 5/4/83. 35) HG 5/15/83. 36) BG 5/18/83.   37) Ibid. 38) WD 5/17/8. 39) HP 5/19/83. 40) WD 5/16/83. 41) WD & WF 5/18/83. 42) WF 5/18/83. 43) BA quoted in RG 5/25/83. 440) BG 9/7/83. 45) *The Central Mass.*, p. 133. 46) HG 9/18/83. 47) BG 11/16/83.

Footnotes, Continued:

Chapter Eight: 1) BG 3/1/85. 2) BG 10/2/85. 3) Myron A. Munson, *The Munson Record* (Vol. II), p. 932-3. 4) RG 6/22/85. 5) HG 11/12 & 11/19/89. 6) HG 2/27/95. 7) *One Thousand Representative Men*, p. 185. 8) Henry B. Wright, *History of Oakham, Mass.*, p. 215. 9) Calvin Coolidge, *The Autobiography of Calvin Coolidge,* p. 155., William Allen White, *A Puritan in Babylon*, p. 220. 10) HS 1/1/96.

102